Fence

Fence

ILA ARAB MEHTA

Translated from the Gujarati original by
RITA KOTHARI

ZUBAAN
an imprint of Kali for Women
128B Shahpur Jat, 1st Floor
NEW DELHI 110 049
Email: contact@zubaanbooks.com
Website: www.zubaanbooks.com

This edition published by Zubaan, 2015

10 9 8 7 6 5 4 3 2 1
ISBN 978 93 83074 87 7

Zubaan is an independent feminist publishing house based in New Delhi
with a strong academic and general list. It was set up as an imprint of
India's first feminist publishing house, Kali for Women, and carries forward
Kali's tradition of publishing world quality books to high editorial and
production standards. *Zubaan* means tongue, voice, language, speech in
Hindustani. Zubaan is a non-profit publisher, working in the areas of the
humanities, social sciences, as well as in fiction, general non-fiction, and
books for children and young adults under its Young Zubaan imprint.

Typeset in Adobe Caslon Pro 11/14 by Jojy Phillip, New Delhi 110 015
Printed at Raj Press, R-3 Inderpuri, New Delhi 110 012

Translator's Note

There is no reason why we should have heard of Fateema Lokhandwala. She is an ordinary girl growing up in rural Gujarat and attending the first-ever school in her village. She is the daughter of someone who collects scrap – lokhand, hence Lokhandwala. Her mother Khatija toils all day, collecting cow dung to make fuel cakes every morning. Fateema lives in abject poverty and dreams of a dignified and proud life that she will achieve through education. There is no reason why we should know of her. This is the story of million of other people in India, people who wish to rise above their circumstances and fashion themselves into successful professionals through hard work and persistence. In this sense, Fateema is an ordinary person who wants ordinary things – a stable career, economic independence, intellectual growth and a home of her own.

These are not unreasonable desires, and Fateema manages to achieve most of what she wants. All that's left is a tiny house, with a little balcony. Taken out of Fateema's context, the proposition seems reasonable, especially as Fateema has earned enough to be able to afford a small house, somewhere. But Fateema is not reasonable, she's not willing to compromise. She wants what is nearly impossible in parts of urban India, and more so in Gujarat, where she lives. Fateema wishes to make her home in a mixed area, where there are different communities. She is a Muslim woman who refuses to be relegated to a religious and ethnic ghetto.

Ila Arab Mehta's gentle narrative of Fateema's pursuit of what seems to be an increasingly unrealistic goal in a secular, democratic country is a severe comment on present-day India. For the literary world of Gujarat, Ila's is an acclaimed name. It would be arrogant on my part as an English translator to claim to introduce an author as established as her. So this translation is not an opportunity to introduce a lesser-known writer who may otherwise languish in oblivion; that is a patronizing thought. My intention here is to let Fateema tell her story beyond the language and region she is part of.

In the world of Gujarati literature, Fateema is one of a kind. Despite there being long and intertwined histories of Muslims and Hindus in the state, the literature of Gujarat shows scarce reflection of this relationship. Mehta's attempt to open up this silence is significant. The modes and implications of representation are discursive and contentious. How can they not be? Hostility, resentment alienation and the rendering invisible of minorities characterize majoritarian attitudes in Gujarat, as they do in many other parts of the country At best, they are ambivalent. Fear, hatred, persecution and separation characterize the responses of those who surround Fateema; in her family and extended community. She and her siblings – Jamaal and Kareem – represent different positions that hint at complexity and the caution we must exercise in concluding 'Muslim-ness' in the novel. Is the author legitimizing one by producing the other, positing Fateema as an ideal by demonizing Kareem? This and other uncomfortable questions that the novel leads the reader to are best not primed by the translator, for they constitute challenges of representation as well as translation in more expansive uses of the term.

Meanwhile, Mehta's translation of Fateema's life, told in combinations of Saurashtra Gujarati, urban Gujarati, Hindi/Urdu and English – all of which are translated here (or not) into what is considered the most global and transformative language of the world – has been far from easy. Anwar's Urdu externalizes his agenda, making his jihad a 'foreign' product brought to Gujarat from Uttar Pradesh, Fateema's Gujarati is a conscious self-fashioning, while Khatija's colloquialisms position her firmly as a rural woman, organic to the life, land and wisdom of simple things. Komal's self-dramatization is most evident in the filmy dialogues that constitute ordinary speech for her. Self-definitions of different characters in the novel are inextricably tied up with different languages and different uses of the 'same' language. This multilingualism of the text, by no means unique to this text alone, is a manifestation of translation and also its test. I hope the English text before you betrays, despite itself, some of this layered-ness.

Rita Kothari
September, 2014

One

It was time for that tiny, hidden dream to acquire a form and a shape.

The thought of making it come true was an audacious one. She dared not do it. And yet, there was a lot she did dare – after all, she was Fateema Lokhandwala, a young woman of courage. It had taken a great deal out of her to simply travel down the bumpy and potholed roads of life. She hadn't had time to even think. But perhaps this was the time – the perfect time – to indulge in a little fantasy.

Every morning, she left the house early. By the time the sun began to silver the grass, she'd already be on her way to work. She lived in a noisy area – clamouring children, bleating goats, cackling hens, ferocious fighting women queuing upto fill water from a common tap.

As pots and words banged and clanged against each other, her two-wheeler would whizz past everything, leaving it all behind. Main road, Mashallah! Like an electric current, the city coursed through her body with the energy of all those people heading out to work – the buses and cars, the heady spirit of urban life! At times like this, Fateema seemed to exist in the future as well as the present.

Despair, loneliness, the deaths of loved ones – everything would recede. On her two-wheeler, she became one with the flow of the city. At Navprabhat College she could look forward to a day filled with tenderness and affection – this knowledge sustained Fateema as she zipped along through the rush and bustle of the awakening city.

Recently, she'd changed her route to work. These days she preferred to ride along the riverbank so that she could see the new buildings coming up away from the city centre. Housing estates were springing up, like this one – Sonkamal Housing Society – which was almost complete. The city's rich had already started to move in.

The buildings had such beautiful names. Sonkamal, the golden lotus. Between two towers was a garden studded with colourful flowers, how beautiful! *Ramniya,* as they say in Gujarati. *Ramniya*…yes, that was the word for 'pleasing.' She had learnt this from Gaekwad Sir when she was in the tenth grade.

Fateema noticed wooden benches that had been set out for senior citizens next to the building, and slides and a merry-go-round for the children. If this is what Sonkamal was like on the outside, what would it be like inside, she wondered.

The two-wheeler whizzed past several construction sites. Some carried notices advertising one- and two-bedroom apartments for sale.

Fateema's heart lurched. She could hardly wait to go over to the property agent's offices. But then she reminded herself that she didn't have the means to buy anything – yet.

She scanned the brick and sand debris and the half-built pillars. Then she tore her eyes away and headed determinedly towards the college. Once classes were over, she'd head straight to the library – she had been thinking of pursuing a doctoral degree.

All this was Fateema Lokhandwala's penance, her tapasya. That was Chandan's favourite word. Fateema's closest and childhood friend was a Jain. She would refer to the fasts her grandmother observed as 'Dadima's tapasya.' Once, she'd even spoken of Fateema's and her studies as a form of tapasya. Fateema quite liked the word. Giving up fun and games to achieve a goal is what Chandan had meant by tapasya.

When Fateema used such words in class, her students found it quite surprising. One day, a bright boy named Manish Dave came up to talk to her after class.

"Ben, you are a Muslim, aren't you?" he said.

"Yes?"

"And yet you look like us, you talk like us." His voice betrayed disbelief.

She laughed. "Arre Manish, I *am* like you. I'm one of you! My teachers and friends are also…" She paused, and then continued, "My religion is different, but I am not."

Another day, a girl had come up to her holding a strip of stick-on bindis in her hand. "Ben," she said, "stick one of these on your forehead. From Fateema you will turn into Falguni." An amused Fateema had taken the strip and put it in her handbag.

She had said to the girl, "Anuja, if I were to carry on being Fateema, wouldn't you like it?"

Anuja thought for a bit. "I don't know about liking or not liking it," she said. "I like you, but my mother says…" She couldn't finish the sentence.

There was no need to. The chasm that lay between the two religions could not be bridged so easily. Fateema had a sense of what Anuja's mother would have said.

"I'm sure she must be good, your teacher, though…" How much unsaid was contained in that word, 'though'. It reminded Fateema of her brother, Kareem, and how he'd he'd slapped her that day. Her cheek still stung at the memory.

"Bitch! You've become an infidel by hanging out with infidels! Mark my words, Islam will conquer the entire world one day."

Was this the same Kareem who used to salute the Indian flag? Who would cry out 'Jai Hind!' and have all the students respond 'Jai Hind!' in turn?

Fateema sighed. Mumbling, "If Allah wills it," she gathered her things up.

Sailing past new homes and colourful gardens, she finally arrived at her college. The wistfulness was turned into a ball and thrown away. Fateema was back to being a teacher. At least her qualifications in History were beyond dispute.

Meanwhile, the dream continued to grow.

"Fateemaben, you have been confirmed as full-time, permanent faculty. You must treat us to a party," Niruben exclaimed as she entered the staff room.

"Yes, how about giving us tea," Vinodaben added, "or some cold drinks?"

"Oh no, surely this deserves more than just tea?" A sudden silence fell in the staff room. Fateema might invite them to her house. Perhaps to eat there? Or would that be over-familiar? Whatever. They were treated to a party.

Fateema immediately ordered tea and biscuits and everyone fell on them with gusto. Then, they began to disperse, congratulating Fateema as they left one by one.

Fateema felt somewhat wistful. If only she had a little house of her own, she could have invited them over.

She found herself back on that familiar road, gazing at all those new homes. It was nothing but an illusion, a sweet dream, an attempt to put aside sorrow and fill the gap with a fantasy built out of words like 'bhoomi pujan' and 'building under construction.' If only she had bought a house earlier,

Ba would have been able to leave the village and come and live with her.

*

Fateema was born in what had once been a princely state, tucked away in the corner of Saurashtra. Long before her birth, the state had vanished from the map – merged into the new nation. The names and even the memories associated with its royal past – the fort, the gates – had faded to become village lore. And the village itself had swelled into a town.

Along with such changes came the Panchayat, and some government offices, followed by a school, established by the Navprabhat Trust, that went from Grade 1 to Grade 10, ensuring free education for the children of the village regardless of caste, creed and religion.

Fateema's father, Maajidbhai, whom she called Baapu and her mother, Khatijabi, whom she called Ba, would say, "This school is Allah's mercy."

Overcoming their initial hesitation, the villagers began to enrol their children into what they called 'iskool', 'nishaal', or 'high school'. They wanted their children to receive the blessings of the goddess of knowledge. They dreamed of their children becoming engineers and doctors.

Of Maajidbhai's four children – Fateema, Kareem, Jamaal, and Saira – two would manage to reach the school 'tame-sir,' or on time. The younger ones were still very small, and often fell sick.

"Arre... arre... who is this?" The words fell on Fateema's ears. She was a grade three student then. She was busy playing thikdi during recess. Fateema, Chandan, Minal – all of them had mastered the art of playing thikdi. The younger children crowded around and watched in admiration as the girls took unerring aim with the thikdi – a tiny piece of stone – and hurled it at the home base. They then hopped on one foot, using the other to bring the stone back. The words 'who is this?' hit Fateema with the accuracy and sharpness of a well-aimed thikdi. She straightened up, mid-hop. They had come from Smitaben, a tenth-grade teacher who had recently joined school. She lived in a nearby town, and travelled to work by bus every day.

Fateema was petrified.

"You study here?" the teacher said, looking her up and down.

"Yes, third grade."

"You come to school in such rags? Hair not combed? Just look at your clothes."

"Ben, she's Muslim," Minal explained.

"So what? Cleanliness is dear to every God. *Cleanliness is…*" Realising that the children would not understand English, she switched back to Gujarati. "Bathe, wear clean clothes, get your Ba to rub oil in your hair and comb it and then come to school, do you understand?"

Fateema looked at her. And then, aiming a thikdi into the distance, replied, "I can only wear the clothes I have. My Baapu isn't going to buy a new dress just for me."

"What does your Baapu do?"

"He collects lokhand, scrap iron, from villages nearby on his bicycle," Fateema said emphatically.

"That's why, Fateema *Lokhand*wala," one of the girls explained, helpfully.

"Does he take your hair with him when he goes?"

The girls giggled. Fateema looked down. Smitaben continued, "It doesn't matter, ok? It's never too late. Try looking neat and clean from tomorrow."

Smitaben left. Fateema's careful mask slipped. She abandoned the game and headed home.

"We are what we are," she muttered to herself. "If they could hear the way I can recite a Gujarati poem – fast and fluent – they'd eat their words."

✳

All mornings are not alike. Living in the corner of a village in a fragile mud-baked house that could fall any moment, Fateema, her siblings and parents knew this truth. This was no profound revelation, but the stuff of everyday life.

Their home was not much more than mud walls topped with a tiled roof. It had two rooms, one without a window. A small-cooking space, a narrow verandah or osri in the front and then a small open courtyard, or faliyu. The faliyu was an all-purpose place for the children – this is where they slept, played, chased cockerels, studied. In fact, that's all they had.

There were three string cots; the rest made do with rag-like mattresses. Fateema and her siblings slept in the osri. Their mattresses were often damp and smelt of mud. But Kareem and Fateema were lost in their respective worlds. They lost themselves in the world of books, and by the age of eight or nine regularly borrowed library books which they read by the hazy light of petromax lamps.

Kareem would bring home books on cricket. Fateema would read fiction and stories about the outlaws in Saurashtra.

Jamaal and Saira would simply play and create mischief. They would chase slivers of moonlight that fell through the cracks in the roof tiles. If Jamaal laid his hand first on the sliver, Saira would throw a fit.

An exhausted Ba would mutter, "Now go to sleep, you wretches. Enough is enough."

"Look at this Kareem, Ba, he is taking the lamp away."

The light would grow dimmer. The family did not have the means to even add oil to the lamp. Darkness would engulf the house. Realising the moonbeams were gone, the two little children would settle down. On such nights, Fateema's stomach would rumble with hunger. She would drink some water and go back to sleep. She would notice through half-shut eyes that Ba gave her own share of food to feed Kareem and Saira, while she herself filled her stomach with a piece of darkness. This did not happen every day – only when Baapu's legs hurt and he missed going to a couple of villages.

Mornings would be quite nice and cheerful though. Ba would wake up early. She would go to the public toilet built by the Panchayat on the outskirts of the village. She would return with a lota of milk.

Ba would remove a couple of cowdung cakes pasted to the wall of the faliyu and use them as fuel for cooking. She would first put water to boil for tea.

The children would wake up and play with water. Tea and roti appeared like a delicacy. Maajidbhai would be ready to set off on his ramshackle bicycle. "Chalo, who wants to fill air in the tyres?"

Kareem and Jamaal would get started on the job, although it'd take a while for the cycle to be ready for use. The children would sometimes go beyond the village boundaries to go to 'the bathroom' but usually they would simply squat near the hedges behind Aalam chacha's house.

"It's time for iskool, you wretched fellows, hurry up!" Ba would give them clothes which were often dirty and torn. Then there was the battle between Ba and Fateema's long, dry, entangled ponytail.

"Ba…aa! You're pulling my hair! Forget it, I don't want it brushed."

"Let me at least run a comb through it."

"It hurts!" Fateema would just flee.

"Wait! Fatee… Oh, she's run away. Look at the forest on her head, but who can tell that girl anything?" An angry and grumbling Ba would return to her housework.

Ba's morning would begin even before Aalam Miyan's rooster crowed. In fact, Fateema's family used to have a few hens and roosters. Some of them got stolen and finally they stopped keeping them.

"To hell with them. Someone keeps stealing them. We will just have to eat daal and roti like the rest," an exasperated Maajidbhai had declared.

As for Ba, her morning began with fetching water, lighting the cooking fire, making rotis for everyone, getting the children ready for school, collecting cowdung from wherever she could, going from house to house in the village asking for torn quilts to sew, and when the children got back from school, providing them with rotis and onions, and at times, khichdi-kadhi.

When the children studied late in the evening, she would watch them with hope in her eyes.

It took Fateema many years to understand that what her parents did to raise them, make them 'Allah's people', was tapasya, their penance. Back then it was Smitaben, rather than Ba, who had seemed the ideal role model. After Smitaben's intial rebuke, Fateema had gone to school with her hair neatly plaited.

School began with the children singing 'Vande Mataram' or 'Ai Maalik tere bandhe ham.' Gaekwad Sir, Jaani Sir, Smitaben, Gitaben and other teachers would pray with everyone else, their hands joined together. Fateema would stand upright and confident. So what if her clothes were unwashed and crumpled, she stood first in class, no?

Two

Like any child of eight or nine, Fateema was not particularly interested in understanding her life and family or the conditions in which they lived. Her Baapu wore a chequered lungi, at least when he was home. Ba sometimes wore a sari, but most often a loose salwar kameez, her head always covered with a dupatta. When other women in the village fasted and participated in festivals, Ba would be busy grinding. This did not seem strange to Fateema. On one or two occasions, Fateema had asked her parents if she could go to the temple for the evening aarti with her friends Naveen, Vinay, Indira and Jeenal. Her Baapu had simply said, "No. It's just not done."

"Our religion is different, that's the way it is," he had added. "Not everyone is alike. Are all trees the same? Some are tall, some are not. These are Allah's miraculous ways."

Fateema understood then that her other classmates Jayant, Martin, and Sumitra were also different. Chandan had whispered in her ear: something to do with Dalits.

"They are from a different caste."

"What do you mean, 'different'?"

Chandan was confused. "My mother says they *have* to be admitted to school. Really speaking…"

Never mind. At their age, who can be bothered with reasons? It was enough to know that, despite being different, Chandan and Fateema, were friends. Best friends, in fact.

It had begun like this. The school had re-opened at the beginning of the new teaching term. Chandan walked in through the main entrance of the school holding her father's hand. Following her was Fateema, holding Khatijabi's hand. There were many other children, younger ones, howling away. But the two girls were quite cheerful. They looked at each other. Chandan was wearing a dress with a flowery pattern, while Fateema was in a long shapeless frock with blue dots. Chandan's hair was oiled and slickly tied, while Fateema's braids branched out like a banyan tree, tied up untidily with an old piece of cloth.

Fateema lost no time in asking, "What's your name?" Chandan looked at her, dumbstruck. Her papa gently nudged her, "Go on Chandan, tell her your name." Fateema giggled, "You just said it. So your name is Chandan, na?"

Khatijabi pinched her daughter, "Stop giggling. It's disrespectful." Drawing the dupatta firmly over her head, she led Fateema away, towards the school. Fateema turned back to Chandan, "My name's Fateema. We are friends, ok?" Since that day the two had become inseparable. They sat next to each other in class, they would eat together at break: Fateema would share her chana, and Chandan her golpapdi.

By the time Fateema got to fourth grade, she had acquired quite a reputation. She was not a big girl, how could she be? But she had a confident voice and a great love for words. She could recite poetry flawlessly.

"Look how quickly she's learned to read!" Khatijabi would proudly remark. "You should teach that Saira something, or she will remain a dumbo forever,"

"You just wait and watch. Both Kareem and Fateema will complete their tenth grade. I am told even girls can find jobs now. Our Fateema will be earning soon."

"Really?"

The grinding mill in Ba's hands came to a stop. A few thousand every month?

"We will not squander the money. Better save it up and mend the walls of this house…"

Lying on a string cot, Fateema looked at the patches of cowdung on the broken wall. Ba had kneaded mud and water into a sort of dough and patched up some parts of a disintegrating wall. Fateema turned back to her books. She was not a child that she did not notice these things around her, but the magic of books, their colourful pictures, her world of rope skipping and playing thikdi drew her back in. She felt sorry that despite the fact that Chandan's father spent so much time in the city, she did not have colourful books.

Are books so easy to come by? Once, Kareem had insisted on going to the Sunday market with Baapu and had brought back a bag full of English books with pictures.

"They're mine."

"No, mine…" The two siblings had a sparring match over the books, hiding away their spoils under their cots. Fateema had attempted a raid, but Kareem had pounced on her, pulling her back by her hair, then dealt her a couple of blows. She still managed to smuggle out two issues of *National Geographic* in her school bag. She went out to drink water during the break, and when she came back, both copies were missing.

Let others cry. Fateema stormed out and ran towards the compound. In the corner of the school compound, Naveen and Vinay were furtively looking at the pictures. Fateema dug her teeth into them and grabbed the magazines back. The two boys gave chase, but when they saw Jani Sir standing at the entrance to the classroom, they meekly sat down at their desks.

There was a teachers' meeting in the staff room. The school trustees made constant efforts to make Navprabhat the leading school in the district. Chandan's grandfather was particularly involved in this project. He watched over everything from an oil painting that hung on the staff room wall. He was dressed, not surprisingly, in khadi – a Gandhi cap and white kurta. Gaekwad Sir was then the school Principal. After a round of tea and biscuits, the conversation had veered towards the school and matters of administration.

Suddenly Gaekwad Sir asked:

"What was the ruckus about some days ago in the compound?"

"When…?" Jani Sir racked his brain. Of course, he remembered. "Oh that firebrand girl Fateema had managed to get some back issues of *National Geographic* from somewhere. The boys must have taken them. This slip of a girl bit them and managed to get the magazines back."

A couple of teachers laughed.

"She's too much! And such a smart student as well."

"I know," Gaekwad Sir responded. "She's one of our scholarship girls."

The school had a number of scholarships students.

"That's all very well, but look at her clothes, poor thing. Fateema has to wear such rags to school." Smitaben added.

"Hmm… did the magazines belong to her? She must be interested, clearly."

"Yes. Her Baapu collects and sells scrap. He must have got them as junk somewhere."

"Why don't we get them for the library then?" Gaekwad Sir looked at everyone.

"But they are in English so…"

"We should start early lessons in English then."

"English? But…"

Without letting the teacher finish, the Principal quipped, "Let's sow a handful of seeds. Something will grow someday. And let's also ask the Trust to provide proper uniforms for the economically underprivileged students."

Everyone nodded in agreement. There were a few murmurs of reservation, but no protest.

The meeting ended.

✳

"English will be taught from Grade Five."

"Wha…? Not possible."

"Of course. The school will arrange for special lessons and also provide books."

"But who will teach?"

"Surely the Principal has figured it out. He wouldn't have suggested it otherwise."

"I'm sure our Jani Sir can teach."

"That dhoti-wearing Jani? And what about that tuft on his head?"

"That lock of hair is his sign of Brahminhood, get it?"

"Good for Navprabhat School though."

"I tell you. Uniforms for everybody, free ones for those who can't afford it. Money is not rare but how many manage to spend it wisely, in the service of education, hanh?"

And so it was that Kareem, Fateema and Chandan began to learn English.

Fateema was growing older, not necessarily wiser. Ba would be busy filling water, mending the walls with patches of mud, making rotis, but Fateema would spend her time doing her sums or teaching Saira.

Aalam chacha's wife Kulsoomchachi visited them to

borrow something. She ticked Fateema off. "Alee, your mother is toiling all day, all you can do is to read books? Khatijabhabhi, what did I tell you? With two girls around, why should you have to slave away?"

"I don't need the girls' labour. They will not be taking the cattle to graze. In fact, Fateema is learning English now!"

A stunned Kulsoomchachi beat a retreat. 'Learning English!' she thought to herself. 'The Kazi will issue orders for the girl's marriage. Then she'll be grazing cattle at her in-laws' house! This Maajidbhai's family is crazy.'

∗

A, B, C – barely were the letters written on the blackboard than Fateema would swallow them whole. Most children watched wide-eyed, but Fateema did not let grass grow under her feet. After a couple of months, she revisited her *National Geographic* issues. She recognized the letters: A… B…. She leapt with joy.

∗

Jani Sir was the Vice Principal of the school. He was tall and thin. He wore a sacred thread across his body and sported a tuft of hair tied at the back. His forehead was smeared with sandalwood paste and his eyes glowed with austerity. Meek and weak students tried to stay away from him, but no one escaped his eagle eye. Spelling, dictation, reading practice – all the students had to go through this ordeal by fire.

Fateema had been singed by other fiery ordeals. One in particular had left its mark on her.

Fateema and Chandan were busy eating snacks during break time. Jani Sir walked past. He must have paused and watched for a while. Oblivious, Fateema put her hand in Chandan's lunch box, took a piece of laddu and ate it. Chandan took some puffed rice from Fateema's box.

"You girls there! What do you think you are doing?" Frightened, the girls stood up. "Chandan, hasn't your mother taught you anything? You shouldn't be eating each other's jootha food like this."

Chandan quailed.

"And as for you, Fateema! You are putting a hand in her box?"

Fateema was about to respond, but Chandan pinched her surreptitiously.

"Chandan, check caste and culture first before you.... This Fateema is... never mind. Just be careful from now on."

Jani Sir left. For the next few days, both Chandan and Fateema ate from their respective lunch boxes. Fateema asked Ba why Chandan had been scolded for sharing her food. Ba's response was terse and simple:

"People," she said. Then she added, "Some are like that."

What more could one say?

Ba wouldn't have been able to explain the fine differences between Hindu, Mlechh, Brahmin and Baniya. She was not even aware of such words.

What she did need to explain, she did so late one afternoon during a scorching summer. The sky was scorched as molten lead. Baapu's tyre had a puncture again. Although Kareem did get it repaired, Baapu was completely exhausted. He could barely stand. Ba had packed three rotis and an onion for him.

Ba left to fetch water and took Fateema along with her.

"Come girl, we'll be done quickly. These little ones will start howling for food soon."

Fateema picked up a pot. People who had moved to the cities had come back home, to what they called 'desh,' for their summer holidays. Cricket matches between the school team and the 'away' teams were played in the compound. The mother and daughter heard laughter ring out as they passed by Chandan's house. Fateema could well imagine that Chandan's cousins from Surat had arrived and they were all having fun sitting on heenchko, the big swing. A couple of them must be holding the iron rods and pushing the swing. *If only I could stand there, holding the rod, kicking the swing this way and that...*

Even if you were used to it, such sweltering heat was difficult to endure. They saw Jani Sir's daughter-in-law, Vijaya, coming from the opposite direction balancing a pot on her head. She was pregnant, and sweating profusely. She said to Fateema's Ba, "Our maid usually fetches the water, but she didn't turn up today."

Ba took the pot Fateema was carrying, "Go, Fatee, you help Mastrani and drop her home." With this, she took the pot off Vijaya's head and put it on Fateema's. "Go home soon," she said to Vijaya. Fateema was not exactly pleased. She mumbled something, but continued to walk swiftly, the pot on her head. Vijaya followed her.

Once they reached the entrance of the large house, Vijaya took the pot from Fateema. "You'd better go. My mother-in-law will say the water is polluted if she sees you carrying it." Vijaya tried to make light of the matter. Fateema turned away. So this is what you get for helping somebody on a scorching day. *Polluted? What does that even mean?* She went back to the village well and took the two pots from her mother.

When they both reached home, Ba said to Fateema, "Do you want to do your homework now? Get Saira to sit next to you then. Let me finish making the rotis."

Ba carried with her no baggage of what she had done, and what she had to do. This is how she carried the life Allah had given her, like the pot on her head, easily. Like a million others who had lived like her.

Baapu would often do his namaaz in the city mosque when he was away. Ba would do her namaaz in the verandah at home. She would make the children join her for evening prayers.

Fateema complained to her mother that evening that Vijaya had shooed her away without even offering her water.

"Never mind, child. We did a good deed. It made Alllah happy."

Kareem stormed into the house. "Why did you take my English book?"

"Why shouldn't I? Baapu brought them for everybody."

He pulled Fateema by her hair and punched her.

"Wretched fellow, may you die. Hitting a sister…"

Kareem fled.

Fateema often sought refuge in another world, the world of Gujarati prose and poetry. From Narsinh Mehta's simple devotion in a poem to an essay about climbing mountains. She told Khatijabi about snow-clad mountains. *Allah, is that true?* Khatijabi found it difficult to believe. But iskool teaches real things, so it must be, she believed. Such was her absolute trust in school.

Why then did Chandan's mother have a problem with the school?

Three

Chandan's house was too large to fit into Fateema's tiny eyes. Green in colour, its entrance was flanked on both sides by stone slabs, otla. It led into an open verandah inside. It's so big! Fateema thought it could take the entire first grade batch. The verandah led into a common room where Chandan's grandmother, Motiba, would sit on a string cot. The room behind her appeared to have a large bed as well as a swing. That must be where Chandan's cousins from the city sit when they come to visit, Fateema guessed. A series of rooms followed, one after the other. What did they fill them up with? Cowdung and pieces of wood?

In order to solve this mystery one had to go inside the house. But Motiba would make Fateema sit on the otla at the entrance. Perched on her cot, she would ask questions:

"Look at you, all ready to go study, shouldn't you be helping your mother?"

Pat came Fateema's reply: "Don't you know that I got the bread this morning? I also helped Saira with her studies."

"What will people like you do with education, hanh? Your father will get you married one of these days to a hawker."

"Not at all. Baapu will let me complete my tenth grade and then take up a job." Fateema spoke with confidence.

Motiba was taken aback. 'What a handful this girl is!' she thought.

Once the school started English classes, Chandan started to throw tantrums and refused to go.

"So what do you want to do then? Stay at home? Come, come, get ready child," her mother coaxed her.

Realising that this would take a while, Fateema took a notebook from her school bag and began revising English spelling. She could hear Chandan whining and the threats and bribes offered by her mother.

"What's going on here?" Motiba bellowed. "Who will marry you, silly girl, if you don't do your matric?"

Silence.

Placated, Motiba continued, "See, all girls in the village have been going to school, right? Look, Fateema is also going, isn't she?"

Fateema stood up. Hesitantly, she peered inside and said to Chandan, "Let's go Chandan, it's getting late."

"Chandli, see? Fateema doesn't even have proper clothes, and yet she wants to go school," Motiba's voice floated out.

Fateema suddenly felt small. Her poverty had never been pointed out like this before.

"So what? At least she knows English," came Chandan's petulant retort.

"What? Fateema knows English?" Motiba was stunned.

"She learnt it in two days. I have not," said Chandan despondently.

Motiba was speechless. Chandan's mother, Pushpaben, could not take her eyes off Fateema. This idiot of a girl was smarter than her daughter?

Motiba descended from her cot.

"This one knows English? Alee Fateema, who teaches you?"

"Nobody."

"You mean you learnt it on your own?" A thought struck Motiba as she spoke, "So why don't you come here early every day? Maybe this girl will also learn something."

Pushpaben had been trained not to question her mother-in-law, but the words were already out of her mouth. "Arre Ba, how can this little girl…?"

"You just watch. Your mother-in-law has some brains, ok?" Motiba cut her off.

Chandan finally agreed to go to school and left with Fateema.

Wordlessly, Pushpavati carried on with her chores. Her son was older than Chandan. He had already been admitted to a boarding school in a nearby town. He was doing quite well, in fact. What was it with this girl? God knows why she'd turned out to be slow at studies.

Motiba empathized with her anxiety.

"Why do you worry so much? She'll be fine, life will also sort itself out."

"I know, but…"

"Children learn from each other, along with each other. Which is why I put Fateema on the job, understood?"

Pushpa felt somewhat reassured.

"Now look the moment she arrives in the morning, make Chandan sit with her and learn. And listen, give away two mamra laddus to her. That'll be enough to make the girl happy. Just do it as soon as she comes. And don't you mention tooshan-booshan. Just say, 'study together.' That's it."

"Yes, Ba."

Satisfied, Motiba continued to swing back and forth gently. All it took was two mamra laddoos to beguile this girl she thought. What she didn't know was that many new directions had opened up for Fateema – English, Geography, Civics,

Gujarati prose and poetry, and Maths far more advanced than simple addition and multiplication.

On some days, Smitaben would bring large maps to class.

"Eh, Ba, come sit here."

No sooner did Fateema return from school, than she would begin her homework.

"What? There's no leisure for death, and you talk of…"

"I see that you have learnt to say 's' instead of 'h.' Good. I'm glad I kept correcting you."

"Oh ho. How clever you are!"

"Will you now sit down for a minute? Look this book says the earth is round and it keeps rotating."

Ba's mouth fell open.

"Haachu?"

"Again? It's saachu, not haachu. Yes it's true. You think Jani Sir would lie?"

Ba may not have believed her daughter, but if a teacher had said so, it must be true. She believed that books said only true things. She would have liked to have heard more, but she didn't have the time.

At times, Kareem would offer a closed fist to his siblings:

"Tell me what's inside?"

"Nothing… nothing."

"Of course there's something."

Ba would tick him off for harassing the 'little ones.'

Kareem would open his fist and announce: "See? There was air inside."

"Where is it? Where?"

"Air is invisible. You can't see it."

Laughing, Ba would say, "This fellow is such an actor!"

The family's poverty lay hidden behind the torn curtains of a theatre production. The fabric would tear on some days.

Once Smitaben made the boys leave the room and took a class exclusively for the girls. This was to talk to the girls about the menstrual cycle and prepare them accordingly.

Fateema woke up one morning, aghast.

"Ba…eh, Ba!"

Oh my God, Kareem, her Baapu, her little brother and sister – everyone was there! Where was the privacy? Everyone surrounded her. Ba immediately understood. She opened up a knot in her dupatta and took out a five rupee note. Handing it to Maajidbhai, she said, "Here, take this. Get everyone out of here."

Understanding dawned upon Maajidbhai. He took the other kids out to buy biscuits. The children, oblivious, rushed to join him. Fateema stared at red stains on her clothes with incomprehension. Ba took her inside and sat her down in a corner.

"Don't wander around in all kinds of places from now." Ba was speaking to her while rummaging around for old rags. But there was nothing to rummage.

"What are you looking for, Ba?"

"Rags."

"Rags?"

"Of course. This dupatta is good, perhaps I should tear it up. Never mind, let me see if there's something else." More than the dupatta, Ba's voice was in shreds. She kept going in and around the house. What could she use? Her husband's pyjamas? But they were still wearable. Kareem's shirt? But he'll kick up a storm. Resigned, Ba said, "You sit here. I'll just go next door for a moment."

Ba went next door, to Valjikaka's house. She returned carrying a torn old sari which she used to make strips. Then she explained to Fateema how to use them.

So that morning Fateema became a woman, and with that, more aware of her family's poverty. In her mind's eye she saw a pile of saris belonging to Pushpamaasi, Chandan's mother. If only she would give away a few to Ba... although would Ba be willing to tear them into strips?

"Chandan?" Fateema was visiting her friend four days later.

Chandan whispered, "Don't say a word about this. Motiba will keep asking you everyday if your periods have started."

Chandan knew it from personal experience.

"Chandan?"

"Hmm."

Fateema was tongue-tied. The thought of asking Chandan for cast-offs made her feel naked herself. She could not speak. She let the matter drop.

✳

Chandan was getting better at studies. Fateema had earned the privilege to sit on the cot inside, and Motiba had stopped badgering her.

She could smell them. An old cupboard stood next to the cot. She could smell the books inside.

"Chandan, what's inside this cupboard?"

"Nothing."

"Is it empty?"

"Let's see." As Chandan opened the cupboard, a couple of books fell out.

"God, so many books! Have you read them all?"

Chandan laughed. "Do you think it's even possible?"

Fateema picked one off the floor. She riffled through the pages.

"We have to go," Chandan said.

On the way to the school, Fateema asked if Chandan would lend her some of the books.

"Sure. These belong to Dadaji. You know he met Gandhiji and also worked with him at the ashram?"

"Really? These are Gandhiji's books?"

Chandan had spotted Jinal by then. "Jinal…" she called. Fateema followed her, pleased with the prospect of new books to read.

Never mind that the uniform she wore was donated by the school, the walls of her house were baked with mud, her food comprised only split gram: her palms were wide open, ready to receive. Fateema moved around in every part of Allah's universe.

Gaekwad Sir had begun to teach English: grammar, sentence construction and short, simple essays. Fateema would begin practising as soon as she reached home. Ba, Jamaal, and Saira would watch her with amazement. Kareem would join her.

"Chandan, will you write an essay on 'My Mother'?"

"What do I write?"

"Whatever you want. It's only five sentences."

After an enormous effort, Chandan managed to write: "Mother name, Mother wear saree, Mother is very good." Fateema corrected her spelling.

"Can I borrow this book?"

"Go ahead," was Chandan's indifferent reply. The book was *Akhri Faisla* (The Last Decision), a collection of Gandhiji's speeches and writings from the Dandi March campaign to his exile in the Yerwada Jail.

What is in this book? Why do you want to read it? Chandan asked no such questions. This did not surprise Fateema. It wasn't just Chandan: most of the students in her class had no interest in history, nor indeed in poetry. Some, like Naveen and Vinay, and even Kareem-iyo did, but they were a senior batch.

✳

It was the first day of school. First period: History. Chapter One of *Ancient India* had been included in the teaching plan, but it had taken the school an entire month to organize the timetable.

The July rain had brought forth little shrubs and turned the vast school compound into a verdant green field. From her classroom window, Fateema watched this pleasant landscape as the sun's gentle rays touched the tips of the grass with light. She was reminded of Gaekwad Sir's Gujarati class.

"*Mehulo gaaje ne Madhav Naache.*"

(A cloud thundered, Madhav danced.)

Gaekwad Sir paused, looked up at Fateema. "You follow, right?"

"Yes, Sir."

Fateema did not mention that in her holidays she had actually read out Krishna legends to Jhamukakaki, Valjikaka's wife! Nor did she point out that when she had read out stories of the Purshottam month to Narbada maasi, she had earned high praise: "This girl is a little thing, but when she reads you can almost see things happening before your eyes." (All this was in lieu of old saris).

Jani Sir came in to teach history. It was his very first class. He moved around in the classroom and spoke. *Iti+ haas* (This is how it really happened) was written on the blackboard, and under that, in large letters *Arya vrat, Bharatbhumi, Bharat varsh.*

"Where did the Aryans come from?"

He pointed out Iran on the map. "This is where they came from, through the Hindu Kush."

A few students studied their history books; the rest were thoroughly bored.

But Fateema was suddenly transported to the Himalayas. So the Aryans came to this country five thousand years ago, hence the name Aryavrat? What was life like then? And what about Iran? It's 'our' religion in Iran, though that was not always the case, right?

Jani Sir continued. "But do remember that when the Aryans came to this part of the world, there were indigenous people here, they were the original inhabitants. Aryans called them 'Dasu' or slaves but they were the real Indians. Theirs was an advanced civilization. The remnants of that civilization are there for us to see at the Mohenjodaro and Harappan sites. The Aryans invaded and established their power over the locals. But they are still the rightful inheritors of this country. They had their gods, and their traditions."

Jani Sir stopped. He reminded himself that this was the eighth grade: students needed only the broad picture.

When the class ended and Jani Sir prepared to leave, some of the senior students stopped him. They'd taken on the responsibility of planting trees and creating a small garden in the school compound while the soil was still moist from the rain.

"Sir, look at this banyan sapling. The gardener says it'll grow into a huge banyan tree."

"The gardner's right, it will. Did you know that the mango seeds you suck on will grow into trees as well, Dhiru?"

Jani Sir did not know that some trees would grow of his history class, as well.

Fateema enjoyed her other subjects too, but History, Gujarati and English were her favourites. Those were the classes she looked forward to most. It was clear, if not entirely comprehensible to her that, "When people come from elsewhere into a country, invade and become victorious, the country does not belong to them. The country belongs to those who were already there before the invaders came. In fact, only to them."

Four

As Fateema sild this way and that between past, present and the future, she couldn't help thinking of the song, '*Zindagi kaisi yeh paheli hai...*' Film songs had become an addiction, thanks to Komal, her hostel roommate. After Ba and Baapu's home, the hostel had become a second home for her, although that was also a thing of the past now. Her current home, the home she was being offered – what was it, she wondered? There wasn't a single window to bring in the universe. Instead, she saw a prison cell with iron bars. She often felt she was being sucked into an abyss.

Terror gripped her: *This room? How will I stay here, in this prison?*

She turned to face the agent, Willibhai, who had brought her there. He had also seemed a little surprised at the place, but had said, "Ben, I suggest you take what is available right now. But put in a request with the Rector: she will give you a better one eventually."

The fact that the building was old was the least of its problems. Away from the city, it was built by a philanthropical organization as a hostel for girl students and working women. Facing the matron's office on the ground floor were a number of toilets and bathrooms. One of the rooms was designated for storage, but eventually used as a room. A little window was the only source of light and air. There was no question of being able to see the world beyond the window.

"Why don't you fill up the form?"

Fateema did and turned it in. The very first line brought a frown upon the matron's face.

"Fateema? Is that you?"

"Yes. I am a Muslim. I teach in Navprabhat College in the city. I am also pursuing my doctoral research."

Struck by Fateema's Gujarati, the matron said, "By the way you speak, I wouldn't have guessed you were.... And what about your family?"

"Ba lives in the village."

"Is there nobody else? In this city?" Different faces, her brother, her friends and classmates living in the city flashed before her eyes. Names formed on her lips, but didn't escape them.

Willibhai came to her aid.

"You see, Madam, the people she knows are scattered everywhere. But I have known Fateema Madam, that's why I brought her here. As such –"

Much remained unsaid 'as such', Fateema thought. A student and teacher of History that she was, Fateema had a sense of her own history. She was a poor student, fatherless, homeless, seeking refuge as a paying guest.

"Very well," the matron said.

The dingy room was all hers. Willibhai did not ask for his commission, but Fateema forced him to accept some money.

Willibhai – William Macwan was 'Allah-sent.'

Fateema's tin trunks went under the small bed. "Have you taken your books?" Ba's loud reminder on a fiercely rainy night came back to Fateema. One of the trunks had the books she taught from and read, as well as a few clothes.

Fateema felt that the 'mohalla' she was now a part of did not feel like a 'Muslim mohalla' – the general sense of backwardness, the unending noise of countless children, men shouting, women hinding behind burkhas – and yet it was very similar. When she visited the homes of the poor to help their children with their studies, it wasn't so very different. There was nothing uniquely 'Muslim' about some things.

Sometimes when Fateema's Baapu left for town, she and her siblings would insist on joining him for a trip to the market. Maajidbhai would relent and occasionally take the children with him. He would show them the mosque and put them in a madrasa nearby, while he went off to do his errands. The moulvi's words from one such occasion had stayed in Fateema's memory. They came back now as her scooter weaved its way through the vast expanse of land beyond the city.

Many, many years ago, there was nobody and nothing: no earth, no sky. Then one day Allah decided to create a universe. He spread a beautiful carpet called the earth. He then arranged a row of mountains on it. He made the sky and studded it with the sun and the moon. He created stars for us to find our way in the dark…

Surely, on this wide and beautiful earth that Allah had made, there must be a small piece of land for me? Surely it exists. Allah must have set aside something for her. It was simply a matter of locating that spot, finding that little house…

Fateema checked herself. Her mind had wandered off while she was navigating a busy street. The traffic had increased and she was stuck behind a truck filled with mounds of sand. She thought about overtaking, but better sense prevailed.

The truck suddenly slowed down, and without indicating, swung sharply to the left. The road on that side was unmade.

Fateema guessed that it must lead to the construction site for a new housing colony. She followed the truck.

Oh yes, she was right! The foundation and pillars of the new building were still being laid out. It didn't seem very large, but it was bustling with activity. Most of the site was fenced off with barbed wire, but there was enough space for the truck to enter. Standing amidst piles of sand, Fateema was transfixed. Ba used to knead mud like this to make walls. Now cement, glass and metal would be mixed and a house will be made.

"Oye... What do you want?" A harsh-looking face appeared.

"Bhai, I wanted just a little information since you are making such a lovely building." Fateema's voice dripped with honey.

"We are not selling. You can leave." A command.

"What?"

"Come back when it's ready." Now the voice held anger as well as authority.

"May I know your name? Can I have a card?"

"I repeat, come later."

Disappointed, Fateema turned to leave. Behind her, she heard:

"Who was that?"

"Some random passer-by. Must be thinking of stealing a sack of cement or two, given an half a chance. Claims to be a buyer..."

Fateema's first instinct was to turn around and strike the man across his face, but she was jolted by another realization. Did she still look poor? She was poor, she was a thief. Of course she was a thief, hadn't she been caught red-handed? A stinging memory surfaced...

One morning, the village children, who had been blissfully sleeping, were startled awake. Arre, who was getting married? Where was the band baaja playing?

Fateema and Kareem, Jamaal and Saira jumped up to watch the procession. Ba's voice followed them, "Fatee, bring cowdung with you, make it quick."

As the procession drew closer, Fateema, Kareem, and the other children had come out running to watch the show. People lined the sides of the road. Arre, arre, is this not a wedding? A baarat this early in the morning? How can that be? Achha, this is some religious function – look at the white clothes, shaven heads… And look! There's Chandan's uncle, her mother – and Chandan herself right up front.

Fateema noticed all this, but soon lost interest. She gathered up some cowdung and returned home.

She was running late. She gave Saira some cursory instructions to help her finish her homework and immediately left for school. There was no point going to Chandan's house. She was anyway busy with the procession. She caught up with Chandan later at school.

"I will not be coming next Friday."

"How come? We have English and History that day." Fateema was surprised.

"Yes, but we have a religious meal that morning," Chandan replied softly.

"Religious meal? What does that mean?"

"Well, it means you eat food…" Chandan was too confused to explain further, but on a sudden impulse she asked, "Would you like to come?"

It was Gaekwad Sir's class. He was explaining a poem from an anthology. He sang the poem:

Holding a hand in a hand
Joining a heart to a heart
On the path of progress
We shall fly away...

Fateema wanted to make a note of the Gujarati word
'*unnati*' for 'progress,' but she was distracted by the conversation
about the religious meal.

"Where should I come?"

"At the Jamanvaar."

"Jamanvaar? What's that?"

"A meal for everybody," an irritated Chandan said loudly.

Gaekwad Sir looked at the two of them. So did rest of the
class.

"Sir, they are talking about food." Amar, who was sitting
behind them, stood up to complain. Guffaws followed.

Fateema and Chandan lowered their eyes. Gaekwad Sir
shut the book he was teaching from and looked up:

"Oh ho, girls, you are talking of meals? Do tell us so we
can also join you."

"Sir, that is-" Amar started, but Gaekwad Sir cut him
short.

"Eavesdropping on someone else's conversation is
unethical and nobody likes a snitch. Don't do it again."

Furious, Amar sat down.

The girls continued to look down with embarrassment.
Teasingly, Gaekwad Sir said to them:

"Why are you so frightened, girls? Scared you may have to
invite me as well? "

The class loosened up and people joined in the lightness
of the moment. Chandan summoned up courage, stood up
and managed to say, "Sir, our religion has something called

'Swamivatsalya'. What this means is that when Maharaj Saheb honours us with his presence, all the Jains are invited to have a meal. That's what we were talking about." She sat down.

"You couldn't have waited till the break?" said Gaekwad Sir. "Anyway," he continued, addressing the class, "Chaalo, take down your homework now. Identify and write about any episode you like from Gandhiji's autobiography. The library has three copies of the book. Make small groups and finish reading it. You can also read in your extra classes."

Everyone wrote down instructions. Meanwhile, it was time for the break and everyone rushed out of class.

When Fateema began walking towards the library, Chandan said to her, "We'll go later, come on. Let's get something to eat. All that talk about food has made me hungry."

As they sat under a tree with their tiffins, like they did every day, Chandan asked, "This religious meal has so many things, I can't tell you… mohanthaal and laadu and gaanthia and papadvadi vegetables…"

"Really? I prefer bhindi."

"But you see we Jains don't eat green vegetables. There are supposed to be germs in them, and by eating them you do violence to them."

"All right, but there are other things, nah?"

"Of course, as much as you want."

"As much as you want, did you say? Really? For everyone?" Fateema found this striking.

"No, silly. Only people of our religion."

"Oh, so how can I come? I don't belong to your religion."

Chandan hadn't thought about this. It's true, Fateema was not a Jain. In fact Dadima didn't even let her enter the house. Dadima mentioned once that it was polluting. She finds everything polluting, Chandan thought. Three days of periods every month. Don't go here, don't go there. Not even Derasar.

But Fateema is so poor, Chandan's heart melted. She had taken Chandan to her house once. Such a humble house it was, cowdung smeared on the walls... *yuck. But Fateema was nice. I passed my exams because she taught me, poor thing. And how will she get to eat such a meal again?*

"You *can* come, you belong to our village, that's why you can come," Chandan said.

"I belong to your school as well!" Fateema was delighted.

"Of course, of course. What is the problem then?"

"What is the problem, hanh? What is the problem? Say it Chandli, or Gaekwad Sir will make you say it five times!"

The two of them burst out laughing.

"Okay, so it's fixed then. You are coming with me for the meal."

"Yes, but Chandan, will there be a lot of people? Then..."

"Never mind them. Listen, I will lend you my chania choli and that mirror-studded green."

"The one your mummy brought? That's so lovely. You'll let me wear that?"

"Absolutely, with a red dupatta over it. Just wear that and sit next to me. It'll be such fun!"

Their excitement grew as they discussed all the things they would eat – sweets, fries, vegetables, dal, papad – but then: "But what if someone recognizes me? Will I be scolded?"

"Not at all." Chandan said emphatically. Then her voice softened and she added, "I mean you do look like us. Just get your Ba to oil your wild hair and make two plaits." Her voice was almost a whisper.

Fateema did not say anything. To think that Ba would have so much oil was an amusing thought.

The subject of the jamanvaar had confounded the poor fifteen-year-old girl. Through her encounter with education, she had blossomed into a confident person. Except for a few subjects like Algebra, Fateema had imbibed every subject to which she was exposed. She even had a neat uniform to wear to school. Thanks to Smitaben's efforts, the trust had made them available for many poor children in the school. Fateema was well known for being a good student. She walked to school with her head held high.

However, the prospect of going with Chandan, as her friend, to this community meal had created turmoil in her mind. Beyond the usual rotla, buttermilk, and a vegetable made with few pieces of potato, an occasional kadhi, and samosas if Baapu brought them, Fateema had never tried other kinds of food. Chandan's invitation had stirred another Fateema within her.

"So what's wrong if I go? I am Chandan's friend, am I not? And the food is free, so why shouldn't I go? Or should I ask Ba? Allah save us all! Ba will say take your little siblings with you, and that would just be the end of everything. A complete disaster!"

Fateema was torn between the desire to go and the responsibility of finishing Gandhi's autobiography, the temptation to eat new varieties of food and the guilt of doing so without her little siblings.

She managed to get out Gandhi's autobiography from the library and bring it home. Her day was made. She lay down on the tattered rug thrown over a string cot in the front yard, and began reading. Baapu was not yet back from work. Jamaal and Saira were probably playing with a stray goat or cow around the compound somewhere. Ba was busy making rotis. Oblivious to everything, Fateema continued to read.

From time to time, she would call out to her mother, "Listen Ba, just listen to this," and she'd narrate an incident or two from the book.

"Everybody says this, live in harmony. Become Allah's person. But the rascals just don't stop killing and stabbing." This was Ba's take on all religions. She would promptly return to her work.

Fateema could not grasp the political context of the autobiography. Nonetheless, she finished reading it. She wrote down an incident that she liked most, and also identified one that Chandan would have liked.

Bas, her homework was done. She also knew which part of the autobiography would be a part of her speech at the forthcoming district elocution competition. In fact Kareem had planned to talk about Abraham Lincoln. Wah! The Lokhandwalla children will steal the day, as the entire district watches!

Fateema warmed to the thought of all the prizes she and her brother had yet to win. As for the jamanvaar on Friday, who would be able to recognize her?

Five

The day of jamanvaar dawned like any other. Aalam chacha's rooster crowed like he did every day. Ba woke up, went and came back from her ablutions on the outskirts of the village like she did every day.

Should she tell Ba? Forget it: she'd be asked to take her younger siblings along. And what would they wear? At least she had clothes: a blue chaniya choli with mirrors, and a red dupatta.

She got up quickly, put her cot away against the wall and finished bathing. Baapu and Kareem were fast asleep. The children had slipped off their mattresses and lay asleep on the mud-baked floor.

Fateema was ready in a jiffy. Before Ba could ask her anything, she was out of the house.

She sat next to Chandan. A number of delicacies were being served, each better than the other. People sat on the floor with leaf plates and bowls. There was mithai, khichu, farsaan and so many other things she hadn't even heard of served from large brass vessels. Fateema watched, wide-eyed. So much food, and such large utensils? Chandan nudged her a couple of times and reminded her, "Stop gaping! Just keep your head down and eat..."

Fateema looked down. Her leaf-plate was piled high with food. Go on, pounce on it. Eat as much as you want.

She reached for the puris, large and fluffy, but she simply couldn't bring herself to eat them.

"Eat! Hurry up." Chandan was worried about someone finding out who Fateema was.

But Fateema was gently picking up food from the plate and putting the goodies away in the folds of her dupatta. She pretended to be looking down, busy eating.

"Fa… Fatee, what do you think you are doing?"

"I will take this home."

"Don't do that, just eat it." Chandan's eyes were filled with fright as she looked around to see if someone was watching. But Fateema did not respond. Chandan noticed tears streaming down Fateema's face.

"Please, please, eat up quickly."

Fateema picked up a piece of puri, followed by the mithai, but the morsels wouldn't melt in her mouth.

"Chandan, Ba, Baapu and everybody else in my house will be eating buttermilk and rotla. When will they ever get to eat something like this?"

Chandan could understand, but she was also irritated. Why did she take this headache upon herself? What if someone found out?

"Fatee, just hurry up. Tuck your dupatta in. Please! Someone will catch us."

Fateema poured the entire contents of the leaf-plate into her dupatta and rolled it up, and tucked it into her waist.

Two figures suddenly loomed over them. "Eh, girl, who are you?"

The two girls pretended they had not heard a thing and continued to eat. Fateema's stomach felt like a pile of stones. Chandan's gut wrenched.

"Eh, I am asking you. Are you deaf?"

A girl sitting next to Fateema nudged her. "He's talking to you."

Fateema had no choice but to answer. She nodded her head, pretending to be busy eating. Her body trembled with fear and embarrassment.

"Oye, I'm talking to you!" He tried grabbing her arm.

Chandan held Fateema's arm and looked up at the face of the caste leader who was quizzing Fateema. She spoke up. "Talkashikaka, she's with me, she's my friend."

Talkashikaka hesitated. Chandan was the daughter of an important person in the community. He asked, "Does she study with you?"

Chandan noticed Amar standing some distance away. He was their classmate, and a troublesome fellow. She realized that Amar was probably responsible for this. What could she possibly say?

"Which caste is she from? Jain?"

All this time Fateema had her eyes lowered. Chandan had not been able to reply, so she must come to Chandan's rescue. She looked up. Her eyes flew to a young man who stood nearby: Vinay Shah. He had completed his matriculation and some years ago moved to another city to continue his studies. Vinay's face was a picture of anger, but Fateema looked him in the eye. His face softened a little. He came forward and said, "If you have finished eating, please vacate this spot. There are other people who have to be fed." Then addressing Talkashikaka, "Chaalo, Kaka. I will handle this." He gently drew the caste leader away.

Whew! Fateema filled up all she could in her dupatta, and she gobbled up the rest as though she was starving. She drank two bowlfuls of buttermilk as well. People gradually began to disperse once the meal was over.

"Stop! I'm going to tell on you now!" A sudden threat.

The girls turned to see Amar. They fled.

The place was crowded. Visitors from other villages had arrived now for the jamanvaar. People jostled and collided with each other. Fateema raced ahead, and Chandan ran behind her. It wasn't easy to run, she had to push her way through people. The exit door, oh God, here it was! There! Now she simply had to reach her home, get back to Saira and Jamaal. Suddenly, she bumped into someone and fell. Out came the dupatta from her waist and all the food scattered on the floor.

A scream escaped Fateema – a wail, rather, as her dream vanished before her very eyes: arriving back home, offering the pile of delicacies to her mother, the little ones would be grabbing goodies…

She fell to the floor, suppressing sobs that kept rising in her throat. She tried collecting the food, now smeared with dirt. Allah…

The person she had bumped into held her hand and lifted her up. Fateema's eyes widened when she saw who it was: the Principal, Gaekwad Sir! Vinay stood next to him. Fateema had read out the *Ramayana* to Narbadakaki. Not once, but twice. She wished the earth would swallow her up as well, as it had done Sita. She'd been exposed as a thief to Gaekwad Sir. *Arre, why did I eat, why did I steal? What will Ba, Baapu, Kareem and everyone else think of me?* She would be labelled a thief in school. Her thoughts crashed around her like boulders, hurting her, plunging her into shame and self-loathing. There was no point in picking up food, but she did not have the courage to look the Principal in the eye either.

"You are not hurt, I hope?" Gaekwad Sir asked her.

"No, no…"

"Very good then. Come here, the two of you." He steered them through the crowd and stood under a tree now.

"Vinay, there must be food left, right? Go son, bring some for this girl. And listen, child, don't you pick things off the ground."

Fateema didn't know where to look. Chandan had noticed that Gaekwad Sir addressed Fateema as 'child' and not by her name.

"Sir, you don't know, but this girl... I didn't want our school to get a bad name, so I let her go."

"Vinay, you think I don't know our own daughters from school? Listen bhai, everybody has an equal right to be fed God's food. That's what compassion is all about. Does a river ask anyone's caste? Does a tree do so before providing you with fruit?" Gaekwad Sir's words had acquired a pedantic tone of a classroom lecture. Fateema and Chandan had nothing to say.

Vinay left, and returned after a while with two plates filled with delicious food. Chandan and Fateema took a plate each and covered it with their dupattas.

Fateema paused before leaving. She looked at Vinay and Gaekwad Sir. Her eyes were filled with gratitude, although she had not yet learned how to say thank you in Gujarati. She left with Chandan, cursing herself all along for her greed. She could throw the plate away, couldn't she? Her hands tightened on it. Chandan's house was on the way. Fateema broke the silence. "Chandan, take your plate with you."

"No way. The food came from my house. You take it, silly. Let me come see you off."

They walked along in silence.

It must have been around one or two in the afternoon. The door to Fateema's house was not shut. Actually, it wasn't possible to shut it. Ba lay on the string cot. Kareem was busy preparing for his tenth grade examination. The little children were at school. The sun shone abundantly through the roof tiles, making visible the holes and dents in the mud-baked floor. Heat and poverty poked at Fateema.

"Take this, I'm leaving the plate here." Chandan looked around and started to leave.

"Chandan," Fateema's voice followed her. "It was nice food, ok?" Fateema felt a lump in her throat, "but don't invite me ever again."

That voice held neither sadness, nor accusation. It was like a dry riverbed. Or rather not quite dry: a hint of water, tears in her eyes, shimmered over the scattered food.

That night, the night of jamanvaar, Fateema curled up next to her mother. She was haunted by images of her collision with Gaekwad Sir, and the exposure of her theft, the food on the floor, and her attempts to pick it up. Unbidden, another image claimed her mind's eye, of her little siblings and parents eating the delicious food. She lay there, torn between the two.

The following day, Gaekwad Sir called her to his office. Smitaben was also present, scheduling the timetable for the next test. Shantibhai the peon was arranging files.

Fateema stood fearfully the door. It must be about yesterday's event. Now she would get a scolding.

"Come in, Fateema." Gaekwad Sir said to her. Smitaben's curious eyes scanned his face. Gaekwad Sir's voice was stern: "Smitaben, look at this girl, she's hiding things from us."

Fateema's eyes welled up. She had not expected Gaekwad Sir to embarrass her in this manner, especially in Smitaben's presence.

"Hiding things? Impossible. Fateema would never do that."

"I am telling you." Gaekwad Sir's voice continued to be clear and authoritative.

"What would Fateema be sneaky about?"

"You do know, don't you Smitaben, that we have a tradition in this school of encouraging bright students from high school to tutor younger students?"

"Of course, which is precisely why we arrange the summer camps."

"Right. So this girl, Fateema, is bright. In fact, she has been teaching Chandan. Surely she can coach grade three and four, can't she?"

Fateema didn't understand where this was all was going. She could see that even Smitaben was at a loss, though she did say, "Sir, Fateema has often helped me out."

"Exactly my point. Yesterday, Tushar and Sanjay's father had come to school. Both boys are behind with their studies, and they need a tutor. Fateema can handle that, can't she?"

"Oh yes, most definitely. She can give them tuitions."

"So Fateema, clearly you've been hiding from us the fact that you are not only a good student but also a good teacher."

Gaekwad Sir was laughing now; Fateema was overwhelmed.

"Now listen, from tomorrow onwards come at least forty-five minutes before school starts. You will be paid a hundred each for the two boys."

"Hundred each?"

"All right, hundred and fifty then, but the results better be good, okay?" an amused Gaekwad Sir replied.

She took further instructions from Gaekwad Sir, and floated home on a cloud of happiness. Three hundred rupees every month? God bless Motiba! Her mamra laddu proved lucky, as Ba would say!

That night, she watched Saira and Jamaal trying to catch slivers of the moon. "I will soon have in my hands not moonbeams, but crisp notes." She imagined herself holding hundred-rupee notes. She rarely even glimpsed such things. But now? Her own money!

*

From that day on, Fateema woke every day before Alam Chacha's rooster. She got ready, quickly gobbled down a roti or two, coached Saira and headed off to school. She stopped going to Chandan's house. She had worked enough for two mamra laddus, although she would still spare time for Chandan during recess.

She had turned into a stern and demanding teacher, just like Jani Sir! She pushed Tushar and Sanjay to study, told them stories, and swore to turn them into achievers.

"Ba, Ba!" Fateema ran towards the house, almost tripping over a little child. She was a whirlwind, her twin braids flying in two different directions. Her Ba was rearranging dung cakes to prepare the evening meal. Smoke rose from the coal fire.

"Ba, we can buy a kerosene stove now!" she shouted. Her words rang out as loudly and suddenly as a temple bell. "Stop yelling. You're hurting my ears," Ba began to say, ready to clip Fateema around the head – but the sight of the three hundred-rupee notes stunned her.

"Hai Allah… where did you get this from? Someone must have dropped the money, go quickly find out who the poor fellow is."

Fateema folded her legs and sat facing her mother. "Aye Ba, dear Ba, this is ours. Our very own."

"Really? Where from?"

Fateema told her all about the tuitions, while Kareem, Baapu and everybody else came in. Kareem ran to the halwai shop, and brought back some mohanthaal. It was exactly like the one they had eaten from a leaf plate. But that was charity. Today, they were eating sweets bought with Fateema's hard-earned money. It was very fulfilling.

"They will give you this much money, every month?" Ba still found it difficult to believe. Sanjay and Tushar's father may do so once in a while, but why would he do it every month?

But Baapu was very reassuring, and an energy ran through the house.

Fateema floated on air. Why shouldn't she?

She had jumped a fence. She had broken the barrier of poverty. She stood on the ground of *Swaalamban* (the word for 'self-reliance,' which she had learnt from reading Gandhi).

Six

Every student from Navprabhat School had cleared the tenth grade! Although this was during the sultry month of June, the village was full of joy. The school compound was festive. No festoons hung along the village lanes, and yet there was an air of celebration everywhere.

Kareem had also done well for himself. He had come first in English and Geography and had been recognized by the school as a bright student.

"Listen bhai, education doesn't only belong to the rich, right? If children study, parents will also rise above their station."

"His sister is also so smart. She even gives tuitions in English!" Parents talked among themselves.

In a nation entering modernity, people were beginning to consider education as important as caste and creed. In Maajidbhai's little hut, Ba was busy doing her chores as usual. She continued to work and mutter: "Son, you must also study further like all your friends."

"Easier said than done," Baapu said. "Education in school may be free but colleges are in the cities. You have to pay money and what about living expenses and clothes?"

"Baapu, just leave that to me. Just give me a thousand rupees. I will go to Ahmedabad and find out," Kareem said.

"A thousand rupees…?"

"Of course… can't you manage that? How will I go then?"

"Now child, take five hundred and find out," Ba replied.

All the children who had passed their exams were huddled in groups of two or three and getting ready to go off to different parts of Gujarat. They were using words like 'Science' and 'Commerce'. words which were beyond Ba and Baapu's understanding.

Kareem was to leave by a bus in the morning. Ba was the first to wake up. Fateema's tuitions had given the house a kerosene stove. Along with roti, now there was the added luxury of dal and khichdi kadi as well. Fateema had not informed Ba, but Tushar and Sanjay's father had given her a bonus of a full month's salary because the two boys had done well too.

Kareem and Maajidbhai were ready to leave. Ba gave them tea and bhakhri. Fateema had also woken up. She went with her brother and father to the bus stand. Kareem was about to embark on an important journey. Fateema put her hand on his shoulder, signalling him to wait. She took out three hundred-rupee notes from the knot of her dupatta and thrust them into her brother's hands, eyes shining with tears of joy.

"This will be useful to you."

Kareem did not, could not, say anything. He tightened his grip on the money and put it in his pocket.

"Be careful, bhaila. There are pickpockets on buses."

"I know, I know." He boarded the bus and Fateema and her Baapu waited until the bus pulled away.

On the way back Fateema said, "Baapu, I also want to go to college, okay? I want to study."

"Who's stopping you? You, I don't have to worry about.

This Valjikaka tells me your Fateema can draw water out of rocks."

Fateema laughed.

Like all those children who need to eke out a living without any support, Kareem had also taken charge of his life and headed to the city. After a month or two he came to visit for a couple of days. He had found ways to settle down. A moulvi had helped him find a place to sleep in somebody's house. He'd got admission to a college and his fees had been waived. He had begun to learn Arabic from a moulvi at night, to be able to read the Holy Koran. Moulviji delivered sermons every Friday. Kareem had begun to help him with that as well.

"How will you find the time to study in all this?"Maajidbhai asked. "I want you to become a big sahib."This was said half in jest. This was a father speaking, a father whose feet were tired from years of pushing a ramshackle cycle, going from place to place to sell old iron and scrap. He thought of his wife whose hands, worn out from repairing walls and making rotis, now sought some rest.

"I'll manage to study. Don't worry about me," Kareem replied.

To Fateema he said, as he prepared to leave, "Take care of the house. Once my education is over, I will buy a house there. I will take all of you there." Fateema was moved. Her brother had become a wise and responsible adult.

Kareem suddenly felt self-conscious. He covered up his embarrassment by pulling Fateema's braids and punching her. "And don't you keep reading like a shethani: you must help Ba. Look at the walls of this house. And this Saira is good for nothing. Work, women, work!"

Kareem had no business telling them to work, she thought.

Every minute of the day was packed so tight that there wasn't a moment's respite. She began her day by reading any English book she could lay her hands on, a dictionary ready at hand. Her father had been instructed to save any old books and English newspapers for her. Ba would say, "It's not going to help if you ruin your eyes like this." This was followed by school, tuition, her own studies.

Because Fateema was bright, she had been instructed by Gaekwad Sir to teach third- and fourth-grade students. But a new development marked her life, so much so that everyone in her class looked at her strangely. It was Smitaben's class on human anatomy, just before Jani Sir's class. She had brought to class huge charts, and Fateema had accompanied her outside class to help her put them back. By the time Fateema returned to her next class, Jani Sir had begun the history lesson.

He was talking about the Moghuls in his deep and resonant voice.

"Rushing ahead with the Islamic flag in one hand and sword in another, these were troops of cruel and violent men. They had pledged to Hazrat Muhammad that they would spread Islam, but their real intentions were to loot and rob peaceful people and return home. That was the beginning." Every now and then, Jani Sir turned to the map to show the pattern of invasion. "The Greeks came from here, the Sakas from here, but they lived like Indians, and merged with Aryan culture, whereas these infidels…"

The class was about to end. Jani Sir closed the book and dictated homework. He informed the class that the librarian had more books that could be borrowed if students were interested in following up further.

Fateema suddenly realized that some people were looking her. Amar said loudly, "Fateema is a Muslim."

Jani Sir was in the process of writing something on the board. He turned around. "Yes, she is a Muslim, but not a member of the savage group. She belongs to the innocent poor who were proselytized. There's no doubt though that she is a Muslim."

Was he saying this to the students or to himself?

Neither Fateema nor the others fully understood the implications of his words, but she could feel the weight of everybody's gaze upon her.

Some months went by. Students found history classes boring. Babar's reign or Humayun's and Akbar's battles held no interest for them. There was no reason left to stare at Fateema because religion had not yet become a hugely divisive force in the village. The students were more worried about exams than about religion.

Fateema had shrugged off her earlier experiences. She and Chandan continued to share the ups and downs of adolescence during recess. Chandan brought Fateema occasional snacks, and news of film stars and cricketers gleaned from the newspapers and magazines in her house.

One day, Gitanjaliben, who was in charge of cultural activities at the school, called Fateema.

"Fateema, let me tell you about a forthcoming interschool elocution competition. Our school will be hosting it. You must participate."

Fateema was not being singled out of some kind of favouritism. The school held regular elocution competitions between different grades and the winners got to participate in the interschool events. Fateema was, in that sense, already a representative.

On the day of the competition, the school compound was choc-a-block with students from other schools in the district.

Some had arrived the previous night. While the girl students stayed at Chandan's house, the boys spent the night at the school. Parents had also turned up in large numbers.

The brief was to describe any one incident from the life of a great man or woman from any part of the world. One by one, students began to relate incidents from the lives of Krishna, Abraham Lincoln, Vallabhbhai Patel, William Bentinck, Mahatma Phule and others. There were also those who spoke about Ramabai Ranade and Kasturba.

When Fateema's turn came, she strode forward, confident, unmindful of her shabby uniform and unkempt hair. Jamaal and Saira, sitting in the last row, watched her with pride.

She described Gandhi's experience of social discrimination in South Africa.

In 1893, Gandhiji travelled to South Africa to represent the case of Abdullah Sheth. He spent some time in Durban preparing and collecting background material. Thereafter he left for Pretoria by train. He was booked to travel first class from Durban to Pretoria. The train stopped at Maritzburg station at about 9 pm. A white man entered the compartment. The sight of a brown-skinned man annoyed him. He marched out and came back with a railway official. The official said to Gandhiji, or rather Mr Gandhi as he was then, 'Mr Gandhi, you may proceed to the last compartment. These seats are not for the likes of you.'

Mr. Gandhi responded by saying that he had a first class ticket for this compartment, and that was how he intended to travel. The official got hold of a guard who physically pushed Mr. Gandhi and his luggage out of the compartment. But Gandhiji did not meekly go to another compartment. On that bitterly cold night, he remained at the station. As he shivered and sat in the waiting room, he asked himself what his duties and rights were, and whether he ought to fight the humiliation he had been subjected to.

Had he wished, he could have continued his travel in another compartment and proceeded to work. Instead he chose to fight for human rights and protest against racial discrimination.

Fateema paused at this point. Following the round of applause, she continued.

This is not where the story ends. In fact, this is where it begins. During the Dandi March, Gandhiji was told that the villagers had refused to give water and food to the police and government officials. Gandhiji spoke of this in a public meeting. 'It is not our dharma to deprive anyone, white or black, of food. Although I have named cruelty perpetrated by General Dyer as 'Dyershahi,' I would rush to rescue him from death, even if I was the one dying at his hand. I would suck a snake's poison out of him. I have done such things in South Africa. I appealed for the life of a man who tried to kill me.' This was Gandhi's non-violence, it was this that brought the English to their knees.

Fateema was applauded for telling stories many people had not previously heard, especially the Dandi March episode. As she stepped down from the stage, Gitanjaliben took her in her arms. Fateema's two students, Tushar and Sanjay, refused to move from her side. When the prizes were announced, Fateema was declared as the second winner. As she came down from the stage with the prize in her hand, Jani Sir said, "Congratulations, Fateema."

Fateema's joy at these words was wonderful. It was like holding three, crisp hundred-rupee notes and rushing home to tell her parents about her first salary. She joined other students in the audience. Jamaal and Saira had not understood much of what Fateema had said, but they were very happy.

"This Maajidbhai's children, I tell you, they're so good," a teacher whispered to a colleague.

"Absolutely. Once this one grows up and becomes a proper woman, no one will be able to guess that she's a poor Muslim."

"These people are different. They live like us, amongst us in the village. But otherwise Muslims are not like us at all."

"Shh… stop talking like that. You'll start a riot here," someone cautioned.

"Of course we would, as this girl just said, forgive even our enemies, but it is not in their blood to…"

"Quiet, please." A hush fell over the group.

Fateema had overheard the entire conversation. *"What does my – our – blood have to do with it? Blood is blood, so what were they…?"*

"Oh ho… this one is a great lady!" Ba was speaking to herself as she lit the stove. She couldn't follow much, but everyone told her that her daughter Fateema had brought glory to the school.

"Allah knows, I don't ask that absent-minded girl to even bring dung cakes. After all, who wants to disturb her while she is reading such big-big books? But, if the village people are praising her so much, she must be doing something right."

Shielded by Ba's quiet consent, Fateema would read away at her books, as she chewed upon kachuka seeds. Chandan's house had opened up a treasure for her. So many books! She ran through books like *Scary Skull* and *The Witch Speaks* in a week's time. Saira and Jamaal had received issues of children's magazines like *Ramakdu* and *Baal Jeevan*. Saira would read

'Bakor Patel' and giggle so much that it would make Ba smile, the house filled with children's laugher.

"Ba, you must learn to read and write," Fateema said to her one day, quite unexpectedly.

"Listen, you crazy girl, how can I learn? At this age?" And using Kareem's words when he wanted to say 'Are you pulling my leg?' she said, "Are you making a fillum about me?"

"Tell me, Ba, wouldn't you like to read Kareembhai's letters?"

"Now see… Why would he write to me?"

"He would, wouldn't he, if you read them."

Ba fell into thinking. The milk began to boil over, but Saira quickly turned off the stove. She brought her slate to Ba and wrote the first letter "K" in Gujarati.

"Here Ba, learn this."

Ba held the pen, and asked, "What is this?"

"Look, don't we say "Koran" by the Prophet? This is the first sound of Koran." An excited Ba drew a 'k.' Fateema didn't have to do much anymore. Saira would make Ba practise every now and then, and make her identify letters as well. Ba must be made literate really soon. Ba had learned to identify letters. One day, Saira wrote on the slate, 'Kareembhai.'

Ba read it out. Saira wrote to Kareembhai and gave him the happy news. But he didn't come running home, nor did he reply.

Seven

"Run away... go... go... run," Fateema almost extended her arms to help.

A bunch of girls, including Chandan and her cousins, Fateema and Jinal, had gathered at Chandan's house to watch a film on video. They were watching *Umrao Jaan*. Chandan's grandmother and mother had also joined them. A vengeful man had kidnapped a nine-year-old girl whose father had testified against him in a land deal. He forcibly took that girl and another away in a bullock cart on a foggy morning. He then sold one of them to a brothel in Lucknow. The scene that played out on the screen was heartbreaking. Fateema bunched her hands into fists.

"Run... run..."

"Poor thing," said Chandan.

The little girl was Umrao, and the film unfolded to show her being groomed as a courtesan. Rekha, the actress playing Umrao, was stunningly beautiful. Rapt and captivated, the girls and women watched, oblivious to the overcast sky outside.

Time went by, and the film wound down towards its end. One day, Umrao Jaan arrived in her hometown to dance. She swayed gently and gracefully to the song, '*Yeh kya jagah hai dosto.*' Umrao's heart lay in the house opposite, where she'd lived as a little girl. As she danced and sang, the beautiful memories of all the times spent there playing with her little brother came back to haunt her. She walked up to the house, and stopped at the threshold. An old woman with failing eyesight recognized her daughter and moved towards her to take her in her arms. Out of nowhere, Umrao's brother appeared and placed himself between them. A pious and religious man, he refused to accept his sister whom he considered to be a 'fallen woman' and slammed the door in her face, saying, "Be off with you! There is no place for you in this house."

As she walked home, Fateema tasted the sweet and salt of her tears mixed with the raindrops that fell on her cheeks. It had been raining gently but steadily. The lane to her house was already beginning to get waterlogged. There was a large puddle of water in the faliyu. Her family was huddled in one corner inside the house. Baapu had not gone to work. He had managed to bring tea, bread and pakoras as dinner for everybody. Fateema joined them. The rain fell harder. Gradually, people fell asleep, lying entangled together. Fateema and her Ba lay awake. Fateema told her the story of Umrao Jaan. Ba could see it vividly before her eyes.

"Scoundrels, they kidnapped the girl? Because she was poor? And they sold her like cattle? She should have run away. These girls are weak, I tell you. If that was me, I would have jumped off the cart. Or whipped him."

By the time they got to the end, Ba was filled with misery and rage.

"The mother should have slapped her son and told him to get lost. Am I right or not, Fatee? This girl is weak, like I said. Otherwise why wouldn't she put her brother in his place? People who sit meekly by get what they deserve."

This from someone with only a basic knowledge of the Gujarati alphabet, someone who spent most of her time making fuel out of cowdung and carrying out chores throughout the day like a beast of burden. Ba's words that day left an indelible mark on Fateema.

Over the next three days the rain showed no sign of letting up. The little village had never seen such torrential rain. The previous two years had been completely dry, so much so that the village lake had dried up. This year, the earth beneath had sucked up water and the lake had begun to overflow.

Fear spread like a rumour in the village. The lake would overflow and destroy people's homes. By the time someone had the wit to shore up the boundary with piles of cement or sand, the lake waters had made their way into the village. And it rained on.

Kuccha houses were knee-deep in water. Fateema's family sat on their string cots. How would a mud-baked house resting on rotting wood and roof tiles withstand the deluge? Ba had somehow managed to cook rotlas in the morning, but by evening the house had become dysfunctional. It was no different in other homes.

Crack. Aalamchacha's house collapsed. Down came the roof with wooden slats. Thankfully Aalamchacha and Kulsumchachi were already out of the house.

Hungry children sat clinging to their parents.

"Baapu, how will I go to school?" Fateema asked.

"Are you insane? How will your Master come in this rain?" Ba answered.

Exhausted, the family fell asleep. Aalamchacha's rooster did not crow the next morning. But Ba's eyes snapped open, as usual. She looked around, horrified. They were almost entirely covered in water.

Soundlessly, the walls collapsed. Ba shrieked. Baapu sat up. They fled from home.

"Baapu, my books!" Fateema suddenly remembered.

"Never mind." The words had barely escaped Baapu's lips when he saw Fateema wading her way into the house. The large plastic bags Maajidbhai used for collecting scrap and school bags were pegged to a nail. She did not waste a moment. Stuffing the school bags into the sacks she ran back to her family. On the way, she quickly picked up the leftovers too – stale bread and pakoras.

Many homes were submerged in water. Some families had taken refuge in the village temple which had a raised platform. The village people asked Maajidbhai also to join them at the temple. With a plastic bag on her head, holding Jamaal with one hand, and Saira with another, Fateema climbed the temple steps. Baapu and Ba followed her, their knees hurting. The family finished eating the leftovers.

The sky was still overcast, the sun almost invisible. It was still raining. Fateema noticed that many people from the village had not come to the temple for shelter.

"Ba, isn't everyone's house submerged in water?"

"Didn't their houses did fall down, Baapu?" Little Saira asked.

What could he say? "Their houses are strong."

"Why aren't ours then?" Saira persisted. Ba was quiet. Fateema tried distracting Saira by pointing out the bag of books to her: "See this? This has the promise of sturdy homes."

Hungry, thirsty and tired, everyone simply waited. The water began to recede a little. Some people from the village – Chandan's father, Gaekwad Sir and Jani Sir among them – had organized food and clothes for those who had taken refuge in the temple. People began to disperse and return to their respective homes.

Fateema's family was also back at their home. The house cracked yet again. Saira had come down with a fever. Ba and Baapu were busy mending walls. Fateema and Jamaal cleaned out the debris. Saira's temperature shot up. She was given some medicine. Two more days went by, the walls stayed up.

Saira passed away.

The wreckage and misery caused by the flood had faded in memory. The village was back to normal. Members of the Legislative Assembly, and Party representatives visited the village. A boundary was built around the lake, but no broken homes were rebuilt, despite many promises.

Kareem came home to attend Saira's burial. He looked the same, but he was not the same person anymore. Fateema wanted to hear stories about college life. But he just glared at her: "Finish your tenth grade. That's enough."

He showed no interest in the awards and prizes Fateema had won for her essays or in elocution competitions. He did play cricket with Jamaal, though.

To Maajidbhai, he said: "Leave this village now. Go and live amidst our quam, where we are in large numbers. Only the quam can help us."

Ba did not take him seriously. Laughing, she said, "Look at you, asking us to leave this place. This village has given us so much! It educated you, gave you food."

"We should have got a lot more. We were the original rulers of this village. Do you know there was a Nawaab here?"

Nobody understood what Kareem was going on about. Why was he so angry?

✳

Two or three months went by. Fateema was only a few months away from her tenth standard examination. Teachers took extra classes to prepare students for the board exams. Navprabhat School was expected to do well this year too. Chandan had been taking private tuitions to help her with Maths and Science, and Fateema helped with the other subjects.

One morning, the Moulviji from the nearby village visited Maajidbhai. Maajidbhai was at his wits' end about where to ask him to sit. Moulviji was a wise man. He was a heavy-set man, and the cot was rather fragile. It was best to stand and talk. Fateema had preferred to stay inside the house. Ba had her head and limbs covered. It was not clear why the moulvi had visited them in the first place.

He extended his condolences regarding Saira's death by saying, "Allah's wish. She is happy under His care." These were not empty words. Fateema could hear the weight of his words from inside the house.

"Maajidbhai, enough is enough. You should move to the next village, that's where people from our quam are."

"How can we, even if we wanted to? Two of my children study here."

"If your kids are studying here, that's not a good thing. And what is this, your daughter does not wear a burkha? You know about Islamic tenets, don't you?"

"Let me see what Aalambhai has to say…" Baapu found it difficult to stand up to the moulvi, although he was clear that his children had to have an education.

"We will take Aalamchacha with us. In fact, we are in the process of setting up madrasas. Put Jamaal there, and put an end to Fateema's education."

Moulviji left. Fateema was unsettled.

A fortnight later, Rajab Ali Rangoonwala came and stood at their doorstep. Initially no one recognized him. Maajidbhai lay sprawled on the cot, since it was Friday. Ba was on the floor, busy putting covers to notebooks and textbooks. All the students whose books had been destroyed during the floods were provided new ones by the school at a subsidized rate.

"Who is it?" Maajidbhai saw a well dressed man in a spotless white kurta, rimless spectacles and glistening black shoes standing on his doorstep. It was bewildering. Rajab Ali's eyes took in the house in its entirety.

Ba got up and left to go inside, signalling Fateema to do the same.

Meanwhile Aalamchacha came rushing out.

"Welcome, welcome, Rajab Ali Sahab, what brings you here?" He looked around, flustered. Jamaal appeared with a muda he had borrowed from Valjibhai's house.

Rajab Ali sat.

"Maajidbhai, this is Rajab Ali Rangoonwala, a well known businessman. He lives in the city." Aalamchacha made the introductions.

"Oh ho, ho," was all Maajidbhai could manage. Maajidbhai Lokhandwala, who went around on a broken bicycle to collect scrap, didn't know what to do with a car-owning Rangoonwala in his house. He just prayed that the muda wouldn't break.

They got past the ritual of salam-alekum-salaam. Rangoonwala's eyes fell upon the English novel Fateema had been reading. He picked it up and read the title, *Pride and Prejudice*. He thumbed through the book, and noticed illustrations, his gaze resting upon one where a man and woman were dancing together. His forehead puckered. Putting the book aside, he asked, "What grade is your daughter in?"

"Jee, she will appear for her tenth grade this year." Maajidbhai's voice sounded apologetic.

"Is she the one reading this book?"

"Jee. They teach it in her school, and she's a keen learner."

"Does she know Arabic? Does she read the Koran?"

"You see, Sahab, this place has nobody who can teach these things. But let me tell you that my daughter says that she will learn and read Allah's message in His language."

"Good, good. Now listen, we will be starting madrasas in our village. Moulviji must have informed you. This westernized lifestyle and irreligious habits must go. You just come there. You know that Islam is in danger."

Maajidbhai didn't know. He simply wanted to uplift his family through education.

"Jee, my older son has gone to the city to pursue his studies. My daughter also wishes to study further."

"Haanji, Fateema is very clever," Aalamchacha chimed in. "She has won so many prizes."

"I know that. But what does 'clever' mean? This education is unIslamic. Now we need to make people like her devout. You must leave this place now." Rajab Ali had measured the poverty of Maajidbhai's family.

Maajidbhai did not understand the full implications, but of whatever little he did, he didn't like it. *Why is he suddenly so concerned about us?*

Yet he was not willing to say anything. Who knows, such established people may have their reasons. Meanwhile, tea arrived in steel tumblers. Rangoonwala eyed his sceptically, but eventually drank it up without letting his lips touch the glass.

"Chalo, I must leave. Do come for Urs celebration next week." Again, a command.

Eight

Once he had left, Khatija came out of the room. Perplexed, she asked: "This bhaijaan has never visited us before. Why now?"

"I don't know about that, but he says the quam must progress. He wants to help us, I suppose."

"Sure! It's the other villagers who rescued us during the floods. How very convenient of him to appear now the waters have receded."

Khatija did not mince her words. Fateema knew that her mother's sarcasm cut people to the quick. "The point of no return," Kulsumchachi called it.

Handing the covered books to Fateema, Khatija said, "There you are. You'll have to write the names. That's your job."

Then she turned to the business of mending torn mattresses.

Later, she again brought up the subject of Rajab Ali with Maajidbhai. "Say what you like, that Saheb has reasons for coming here."

Maajidbhai laughed.

"You are so naïve! What would interest him in this run-down house? Hidden treasure stashed in the crumbling walls, you think?"

Resigned, Khatija shook her head. "You are a simpleton, Allah's man. Not everybody is like you."

A thin smile played upon her lips as she continued, "Who cares if he's rich? It's our daughter who reads English. He was so stunned by that!"

Maajidbhai stretched himself on the cot, and looked up at the sky. "Of course. You know, when I go into town and see young girls riding two-wheelers and going to study, I dream about Fateema doing the same."

Fateema was busy pressing his feet. Her hands froze. *Would Baapu really let me go to study, like Kareembhai?*

"Although Rajab Ali says girls in our quam shouldn't be studying so much," Maajidbhai concluded.

✳

Struggling to make ends meet, Fateema's poor and hard-working family had put little Saira's death behind them. Sometimes Khatija's hands stilled in mid-air while making dung-cakes. But then she'd just go back to the job in hand.

One such morning, Alamchacha paid the family a visit. He was grinning from ear to ear and held a packet in his hands. "Maajidbhai, there's a letter from Rajab Ali."

Maajidbhai was busy pumping up his bicycle tyre. Without looking up, he asked, somewhat absent-mindedly, "Who did you say? Rajab what? Oh, yes, yes. The one who came here, of course."

"You have forgotten him or what?"

"No bhai, no, how can I forget him? He honoured poor people like us with his presence…" There was a slightly facetious note in Maajidbhai's words.

"Excellent. He has not forgotten you either. He has invited all of us to attend the Urs celebrations."

"Urs?"

"Why? Didn't he mention that to you?"

"But Aalambhai, these kids have exams. How can we leave at this time?" Maajidbhai was pleased with himself for using the word 'exam.'

"Also, we don't know anybody there," Ba went on. "It'll cost us to go and come back – and besides, we don't have good clothes. Just forget it."

"Come on, Maajidbhai. It's such an honour, and it's just a matter of one or two days."

Aalambhai's persistence, Jamaal's excitement at the thought of attending Urs and the prospect of donating something in Saira's name made Maajidbhai finally relent. He decided to take the kids with him.

What would interest him in this run-down house? Hidden treasure stashed in the crumbling walls, you think? The answer was apparent as soon as Maajidbhai's family reached the town where Rajab Ali lived.

Arre, how had he not seen the 'treasure' Rajab Ali was after? Rajab Ali had clearly done his homework on Maajidbhai's poverty and his young, jewel-like daughter.

The Urs festivities were in full swing. Rajab Ali had made arrangements for Maajidbhai and his family to stay in an old but pucca house. Fateema and Jamaal were awe-struck by the house. Maajidbhai sat down on a cane chair, and found the exhaustion that had built up over years draining out from his body.

"Valjikaka's house also has a sofa like this." An overjoyed Jamaal scampered to see every nook and corner of the house.

What a lovely house, Maajidbhai was thinking. A verandah, strong walls, otlas to sit on, two rooms, a kitchen, and a balcony. It'd be wonderful to live in a house like this. Fateema broke his reverie, alas.

"Baapu, Gaekwad Sir has given me leave for only two

days. He said he was letting me go because it was a religious occasion, but now I really need to get back."

"Don't worry, we will return soon."

Soon after, Rajab Ali appeared, along with a servant carrying tea, bread, butter and hard-boiled eggs.

Maajidbhai quickly stood up.

"Salaam Alekum."

"Alekum Salaam," Rajab Ali replied, signalling his servant to put everything on the table. Plates were laid out. Such arrangements were intimidating for Maajidbhai's family. Rajab Ali asked Fateema to start serving. While Fateema carried out his orders, her eyes implored her father to inform Rajab Ali that they had to leave soon.

Sipping his tea, Maajidbhai said to Rajab Ali, "We would like to take your leave Saheb, it's already been two days."

"Come now, Maajidbhai, how can you talk of going? In fact you must call Bhabhijaan here as well!"

"Here? But…" An astonished Maajidbhai didn't know what this meant.

"I mean it. You can settle down in this town and also consider this as your daughter's house."

The meaning of his words very slowly dawned upon Maajidbhai, but he wanted to confirm. "I am not sure I understand you."

"What is there to understand, bhai? You see, my brother has a son named Aslam. He is into the business of transport, trucks and taxis. Let's get him and Fateema married, that's all."

Maajidbhai was dumbfounded. Fateema and Kareem's teachers had been talking to him about making his children engineers, doctors, lawyers. Where was marriage in all this? He had not given a thought to his daughter's marriage. In any case, how old was she? Fifteen? Sixteen? Oh Allah, was it time to get her married? And this house, could it actually belong to his family?

"Now listen, this is the way it's going to be. From now on, Jamaal will address you as Abbajaan. And you will move to this place. As for Bhabhijaan, she will have such a restful life here. We will also find something decent for you to do. You can't go on collecting and selling junk."

Rajab Ali Rangoonwala had created rangeen – colourful – dreams.

Maajidbhai was choked with emotion. He saw before his eyes an end to all his miseries. His raised his eyes to the heavens. "Allah, has the time come then?"

"Here, have your food. And do call Bhabhi over. Once my brother and Aslam meet you, we can consider the matter final."

With this, Rajab Ali left. Fateema felt as if her world had come crashing down.

She looked Maajidbhai straight in the eye. "Baapu, why didn't you speak up?"

"What should I have said, beti? Just see how kind Allah is being to us."

"So? Are you planning to marry me off, Baapu? Didn't you hear? He wants me to do nikaah with a taxiwallah." Fateema broke down.

"Say Abbajaan, not Baapu," Jamaal interjected. "And this house will be yours, silly. We will finally have a proper house of our own."

Fateema's gaze turned to the house. It was very nice, indeed. But she asked, "Do you want such charity? Our home is made through toil and sweat."

Ignoring her comment, Maajidbhai said to Jamaal, "Go call up your Ammi. Tell her, she should come here now."

The women Fateema had seen during Urs flashed before her eyes – locked behind burkhas, surrounded by five or six children, dragging their feet behind their husbands. *No, that's not for me*, she thought. *I want to become a teacher. I want to study.*

"Abbajaan, may I go and call up Ammi?" Jamaal asked.

His eyes shone with joy. "That room upstairs is mine, ok? No giving that to Kareembhai."

"Yes, yes. Now tell your mother that it's Fateema's nikaah, so she must immediately come here." Maajidbhai seemed to have made his plans. A nine-year-old Umrao Jaan came to Fateema's mind.

Run, run away... her heart had screamed then, as it did today. And Ba's words: "These girls are weak, I tell you. If that was me, I would have jumped off the cart. Or whipped him"

But we will have a house of our own. Baapu will have a good job. Kareembhai will go into business. Fateema, your entire family will be happy. And after all, every girl has to marry some day or the other. Just look at your father, how happy he looks. Go on, say yes.

Meanwhile the servant returned to pick up the crockery. He had a brief chat with Fateema.

Jamaal was getting ready to leave, but Fateema immediately volunteered.

"Baapu, let me go make the call. Jamaal won't know how to dial." The phone call had to be made to Valjikaka's house. Fateema's voice quavered.

"Will you? Okay, let me give you the money."

"No need. I have money."

Fateema quickly left, carrying with her one of the textbooks that had the school stamp and phone number on it.

There should be someone in school, Gaekwad Sir or

Jaani Sir. Or maybe it's recess now. Fateema thought hard as she walked.

It was an unknown town and she had to make the call without letting Rajab Ali know. She asked for directions to a school in that area. It was not very far. She saw a clerk in an office on the ground floor.

"I need to make a call."

"Students are not allowed to use the phone."

"I am not a student of this school. I am from Navprabhat School and that's where I need to phone."

She strategically put a ten-rupee note on the table. A surprised clerk opened the lock on the telephone. Fateema asked the operator to put her through to the school.

"Hello?" came a voice at the other end.

"Hello, Jaani Sir? This is Fateema. Fateema Lokhandwala."

✳

"You? I don't know what to say to you. Did you go there to attend Urs or to get your daughter…"

"Enough," Maajidbhai interrupted Ba. "I told you before that I found his proposal reasonable."

Ba knew that Rajab Ali Rangoonwala was intimidating.

"Had I been asked to do a nikaah, I would have certainly said yes," Jamaal butted in. Everyone laughed.

Ba pinched his cheek affectionately, "Grow a moustache and beard first. Thinking of nikaah already!"

"Of course I will. But Ammi, I mean Ammijaan, had you been around you would have noticed how many of our kind of people were there. Right, Abbajaan?"

"What is this Ammijaan-Abbajaan thing? You had trouble calling me even Ba earlier, all you did was to yell!"

"At least listen to what I am saying," an impatient Jamaal

responded. His mother was digressing. "You would have agreed, too, if you saw the house. One room after another, a terrace as well."

"Really? Is that true, Fatee?"

"Yes." Fateema was monosyllabic. She had a lot of catching up to do. She had missed classes and had brought Jinal's class notes home to copy them out.

"Ammi, you should have seen the size of the mosque. On Fridays, the entire mosque gets filled up."

"Jamaal, shouldn't you be studying now?" Fateema reminded him.

"I forgot two of my books there," he laughed sheepishly. "But never mind, let me finish talking, okay? Ammi, our roof is so rickety, but the terrace there was so good, I went right up and could see the entire village!"

Fateema stopped writing. She began to think about the house. It was not as large as Chandan's. Fateema used to receive two mamra laddus at Chandan's, whereas this house provided them all meals of the day.

On top of that, the taxiwallah already had a wife. Fateema had come to know this through her furtive conversation with the servant. Words from the past rang in her ears, "Your father will marry you off to some hawker or driver."

Fateema sat up with a start. Back then, and even now, Fateema had the same response. However it was Ba's words that fell on her ears next: "That sheth thinks he's so smart. But we are no idiots either. This boy Aslam is neither very educated nor successful. All this giving of the house is a cover-up." Ba didn't know about the first wife: God knows what kind of wrath that would have unleashed.

An exasperated Maajidbhai turned over on his side.

"Give it a rest, will you? The matter's over now."

"I know. When Jani Sir created a storm, I was so scared. He tells me, Fateema has phoned, you come with me. Thank heavens we reached on time."

The matter was over. Or was it? Perhaps for Jamaal it had just begun. The day they arrived home, he had raised his voice at dinnertime. "What is this? Is there no mutton pulao? What do I eat this ghaasphoos with?"

"Shut up. When did we have mutton pulao before? Just eat what you have," Ba shouted.

But Jamaal found it difficult to swallow even one morsel. The buttermilk appeared too watery to him. Rajab Ali had provided such thick sweet lassi with a fine layer of cream on top! The few days of luxury that Jamaal had experienced had unsettled him. His parents reminded him to do his 'layson' or homework all day. But Jamaal vented his anger against Fateema who had set such standards, "I am not going to do it. I am not like Fatee."

He somehow got through his dinner. As he lay on the string cot, he gazed at the moon. Moulvi had mentioned something about the beauties of heaven. Jamaal had understood the imagery, which now haunted him, in flashes. His thoughts turned to Aslam. *How good he looked, with a red handkerchief around his neck and a paan in his mouth. How did Jani Sir come to know where they were to bring them back here? Had I stayed on, I would have been driving a taxi. Aslambhai plans to go to Bombay. I could go with him. He says he will become a movie star.*

Jamaal's fantasies weighed heavy; he sat up in bed. His cot creaked and startled Fateema.

"What's the matter? Mosquitoes bothering you?" she asked.

"I can't sleep."

"Look at the moon there, see how much beauty Allah has created. Just dwell on it, you will fall asleep."

Fateema had no idea what Jamaal was dwelling upon. Not mosquitoes, but doubts nagged him.

"Fatee, you know the way Jani Sir came and fetched you? Do you think he'd do that to me as well, if I had gone?"

"Why, you think he has all the time in the world or what? He did that in the first place because…." Except Ba and Baapu nobody knew of Fateema's secret. It was dangerous to let Jamaal know. So she checked herself.

Jamaal didn't need to know more. With his doubts allayed, he could go to sleep. What must Aslambhai be doing? Watching TV?

The following morning, Fateema was ready at the crack of dawn. She had not met Chandan in a long time. Her father was in bed. He showed no intention of going to work.

"Is there a puncture in your bicycle?"

"No. Just generally."

Fateema realized that her father was a tired man now. His feet were swollen from constant cycling. Bas, it was a matter of one or two more years. Once Kareem finishes his education, they would all move to the city. *I will study there, so will Jamaal.*

Once Fateema had left, Jamaal asked his father for fifty rupees.

"Fifty? What for?"

"I want to go back."

"Back where? You can't keep missing school like that."

"I want to go to the Urs."

"Arre but listen…" Jamaal was in no mood to listen. In the afternoon, when Maajidbhai was napping and Ba was out finishing up the chores, Jamaal stole the money and left.

"Don't worry about Jamaal, Maajidbhai. He's fine," Aalamchacha brought reassuring news a few days later.

"But his studies…"

"What studies? Aslambhai told me that Jamaal is learning to drive and repair vehicles. Let him be. The boy seems to have found work of his liking."

"All right then." Maajidbhai gave up. Ba, however, insisted that Baapu bring Jamaal back. Maajidbhai went around the villages, collected some scrap and returned.

"I know I should have brought home that bigger scrap."

Ba muttered something. The matter was put to rest.

Nine

It had been a while since Jamaal had left home and now it was time for Fateema to do so. It was time to leave Ba and Baapu, the kitchen and osri. Fateema did not think of this as an experience unique to her. In the English fiction she had read, she'd come across stories of girls studying in boarding schools, of poor boys and girls curling up on bitterly cold nights, succumbing to pneumonia and tuberculosis. These brought tears to her eyes but she was secure in the knowledge that she could sleep every night with her head resting on Ba's lap. Now this would change. The time to leave home was also the time to find a place in the wide, unknown world. At least Chandan could stay at her uncle's house.

It was time to get off the train. She looked around, puzzled. Vadodara junction was a hub from where trains left to go off in many different directions. Which way should she go?

Kareem had arrived at the station to receive her. He looked angry.

"Why did you come? You should have stayed with Abbajaan at home. I had told them not to send you. Didn't Ammijaan tell you that?"

Fateema attempted to smile. "Since you came, I also came, right?" But Kareem was far from amused. He doesn't like my coming, Fateema thought as she walked out of the station with him. He would have liked me to stay at home, earn money, look after Ba and Baapu. He visited them when Jamaal fled from home, but he did not help in bringing Jamaal back.

He had said to Ba in a threatening tone, "No sending Fateema! She's had enough education."

But you think Ba was the sort to feel threatened?

"Fatee, what is that place called where girls go to study?"

"College."

"That's it. Smitaben came over especially to tell us. If other girls from the village go there, why can't Fatee? And she says there's a place to stay as well."

"Hostel."

"That's it. These wretched names are hard to remember. Let her study. If she doesn't, she'll just come back." Ma closed the matter with her classic simplicity. "Jamaaliyo didn't come back either, did he?"

Junior College classes had not yet begun, but hostel rooms had to be reserved. The two siblings asked for directions and left for the hostel. Kareem had borrowed his friend's motorbike. Fateema rode pillion. He asked her to hold him tight.

Zoooomm… Fateema felt lifted into a new world suddenly. Zigzagging his way through the traffic, Kareem appeared to her like a film hero. Fateema also noticed girls riding two-wheelers. She remembered Baapu's words, "My daughter could ride a two-wheeler…" She'd make Baapu's wish come true, just you wait.

Fateema and Kareem had reached the hostel. Kareem parked his bike and they entered the building. The rector's office was on the ground floor. The sign said 'Manorama Gandhi'.

The door was wide open. There was no need to go through a magical labyrinth led by a peon. Manoramaben was going through a pile of applications.

"Madam, we're here for admission into the hostel."

"Sorry, we have no places left. Next term please."

Kareem got up to leave.

"Chalo, Fateema."

Manoramaben looked up, her eyes scanning both of them.

"See, Madam says it's not possible," Kareem told his sister. "Didn't you hear? Let's go now."

But Fateema didn't budge. Manoramaben anticipated entreaties and arguments. Preparing herself, she said: "Look, don't waste my time. I have about a hundred applications to read."

An impatient Kareem was already at the door. Fateema turned around and said to him, "Please wait outside for a while. I need to talk to Manuben."

Manoramaben was taken aback. Fateema also realized that she had sounded too familiar. Apologetically, she said, "Sorry, I have been reading Gandhi, so I said Manuben by mistake."

Manoramaben gave her a steady look. She smiled a little.

"Madam, my school Principal gave me a note of recommendation." With this she handed over Gaekwad Sir's letter to the hostel trustee. Manoramaben read the letter.

"All right, fill up the form."

Kareem entered the room for a second time. He saw Fateema filling up the form.

Name: Fateema Lokhandwala

"Are you Muslim?"

"Jee. But I studied in Navprabhat School. So did my brother Kareem here."

As far as Kareem was concerned, the time to protest had gone. It was time for Fateema to be admitted to a hostel.

Matushree Taramati Gandhi Hostel. A three-storey building. This is my home for the next few years. Fateema's heart swelled at the thought. She was also somewhat wistful.

Manoramaben told Fateema eventually that she was indeed called Manuben. She also laid down the rules firmly.

"No non-vegetarian food is allowed in this hostel. Our kitchen provides a simple meal every day. You need to make an advance payment of six months towards the Mess. Food consists of dal, rice, roti."

Fateema's thoughts strayed to her parents far away. Baapu, who carried his home-cooked food and rotis. His 'brood' somehow swallowed rotis with buttermilk and ran to school. Manuben, this is plenitude. Sometimes, Fateema would lie down on her hard mattress, think of home and shed tears. But that time was over, and Fateema had begun to understand city life.

Fateema had been allocated a tiny room that was part of a corridor outside Manuben's office. Next door to the office were the toilets. Adjacent to this area was a waiting room with an old sofa and some tables. Hostel girls also used it to play indoor games or simply sit and chat.

The hostel had strict rules. Manuben was a stern disciplinarian. By nine in the evening, everyone was expected to retire to their respective rooms. Each room had two people. Although Fateema had not been told why she wasn't sharing a room with anyone, it wasn't too hard to guess. It was unlike Fateema to raise questions and be confrontationalist – and in any case, there was freedom in being alone.

College commenced.

Kareem's friend Anwar had come to take her to college. Fateema had not expected this.

"Where is Kareembhai? Why didn't he come?"

"He had to go to Bharuch for some work. So he asked me to drop you."

The two of them stood next to Anwar's bike.

"Bharuch? What work did he have there?"

"I don't know, but he's back in a day or two. Chalo, I am here so I can drop you, right?"

Anwar rode his bike, while Fateema took an auto to college. Fateema was looking forward to her first day, although she was somewhat saddened by Kareem's absence. Had Kareem seen so many girls studying in college, he would have softened. At the college gate Anwar remarked, "Colleges like this spoil girls."

"What do you mean? 'Spoil' in what sense? They have to study somewhere," Fateema was genuinely taken aback.

"People like you will not understand. Your heads are filled with the so-called English education – all kinds of rubbish such as History and Geography. Get rid of that first."

Fateema laughed. "Anwarbhai, you sound so serious, for a minute you had me believing that you were genuinely against education."

"But I am."

"Arre, Kareembhai is a science student, isn't he? And that's ok?" Fateema persisted.

"Yes it is, because science helps." Anwar stopped himself.

There was no time for a long discussion. Students had begun to enter the building in small groups. Many girls, accompanied by their mothers, stood near the notice board. Fateema was all alone and yet a new energy surged within her.

She entered the college building. Life took a different turn.

✳

Life took a different turn. Just as well he came here, Kareem thought. And then he corrected himself. No, Allah had brought him here and put him in touch with Anwar the very next day.

Back from Bharuch, Kareem went to deposit the cash in the bank. He had managed to collect a substantial amount.

On his way to Anwar's, he was thinking: what would I have done without him? I would have been living in this rotten neighbourhood, deprived of religious norms and practices. Inshallah, I won't have to live here for long.

There were no laboratory sessions today. The streets overflowed with traffic. Boys and girls appeared gay and joyful, chatting away and walking. Disdainfully, he turned his gaze away from them.

Anwar had arranged a meeting with a moulvi from Bombay. They were supposed to meet in a corner inside the mosque. Since the meeting was scheduled at noon, and it wasn't Friday, no other visitors were expected. Kareem was there on time.

The moulvi looked to his left and right. There were ten young men. They would do, he thought. 'Salaam Alekum' and 'Alekum Salaams' were exchanged. They all sat down as if for namaaz.

Silence. The young mean looked at the moulvi with anticipation. They were ready for a jihad against anti-Islamic regimes. Their guiding star had now specially arrived from Bombay. They were to be martyrs in the service of Islam.

Anwar made a start. "All these are members of the Islamic Youth Association. This is Javed, that's Kareem…"

The moulvi acknowledged each one with a nod. Then he turned to Anwar and asked,

"Islamic Youth Association – what a sacrilege of a name."

Anwar smiled. "Zakir Sahab, this is only a façade. We don't want to draw the police's attention to our group. We do 'social service.' We help old people. For instance, we sent money to Kareem's Abbajaan. We got Javed's father treated for his illness. We have established a name for ourselves by doing public service."

The Moulviji was convinced, although he did say, "Anwar, social service need not be a façade. The principle of 'khairaat' in our faith is all about helping the poor. It is Allah's command to provide for the aawaam."

"We are ready to act on every command made by Allah."

"Patience. For now, we stay with social service and training. I merely wanted to see your preparedness for the training. Two of you will be sent next year for training. We will need funds for that. And yes, it is time we take the women along with us."

Kareem had passed his twelfth grade exams with good results. Baapu had said to him with some disappointment, "Kareem, you have the potential to come a doctor. I wish you had put in some extra effort."

"I know, Kareembhai," Fateema added, "if I was as good as you in maths and science, I would have chosen to be a doctor."

"Rubbish. Science is not only about becoming a doctor. I am not interested in being one."

"So what are you going to study now?"

"Pure Science: BSc."

No one knew what to say to that, so the matter was closed.

Fateema was, of course, hugely happy to get rid of maths and science by her eleventh grade. She did try but like a classic Arts student, she just could not get along with Physics.

Subjects like literature, social science, and history brought her a great deal more joy.

Fateema, like Kareem, completed her twelfth grade, and continued to study in the same girls college for her B.A. Kareem disapproved of the fact that there was a co-educational college with girls and boys right next to Fateema's. He also did not like that male professors taught female students in a girls' college. But Anwar had prevailed upon Kareem to let Fateema study. He said to him, as usual in Urdu, "*Auraton ko saath rakhna, padi likhi auratoki aaj khaas* demand *hai*: We need educated women."

"Ok, Anwarbhai, *jaisa aap kahein*."

"How do you find college? Do you like it?"

Fateema often asked herself this question. Who else would, after all? She was now in a degree college.

There were about fifty female students in class, each better looking and more elegant than the other. Allah's spectacle. A few were like her, rural Gujaratis, but most were urban. The ones that came from well-to-do families had groups of their own. They would often go to the movies after class. This included Chandan. Their paths had diverged.

After lunch, Fateema would largely be alone, and she'd spend the time studying in the library. At such times she would ask herself, "How do you find college? Do you like it?" Why not? She had been taken by an angel to the sky, and asked to choose a colour from a rainbow. All of them. She liked college in its entirety: the girl students, the education, the professors, the library...

"How do you find college? Do you like it?"

Arre wah! Kareem was asking her this question, finally? Her brother, Kareem, who would pull her braids, punch her, grab her roti and scamper, that brother had now ceased to exist. Sporting a beard, he looked severe. He was also a well-built man now. His eyes behind the thick, black-framed spectacles looked at the world pointedly.

"It's nice, and you know, Kareem, it's not at all difficult. I use reference books since my English is…" Fateema noticed that Kareem was not listening.

"Never mind all that. Are there any Muslim girls? Be sure to make friends with them."

"But why? They are my seniors. And you think friendship is that planned?"

"Don't worry. Just do as I say." With this, he strode away.

Fateema wanted to tell him she was now secretary of the History and Social Sciences Association and the following month she would be giving a talk entitled 'Peace and Islam'.

Who could she share these things with? She and Chandan met every day even though they were in different sections. Chandan had opted for Hindi and Gujarati electives, while Fateema had taken History, English literature and Anthropology. People found this combination quite surprising.

She often met Chandan during the break. They did not share each other's food anymore, although Chandan insisted on sharing a pizza with her in the canteen. They would sometimes sit on the college lawns and chat. Chandan's cousins studied in the same college. They would go by and say hello to both. Chandan was, even today, a special friend.

"I have enrolled for cooking lessons," she would declare or, "I'm going to start English speaking classes from today."

"You look so different now, Chandli." Chandan loved it when Fateema used the old endearment.

"I do, don't I? My kaki is making me do all this. She lives

in Africa. She has also lived in London. She wants me to be transformed from a desi girl to a videshi girl." Chandan flaunted her new hairstyle. They laughed delightedly.

Chandan had a stylish 'stepcut' haircut, whereas Fateema had remained Fateema. The same thick, curly and unruly hair disciplined by elastic bands into braids, and her fair skin was make-up free.

One day, Chandan said to her, "A boy from my kaki's family will be arriving from London. If he likes me, yours truly will go to London!"

"If he likes you, why do you say that? What about your liking *him*?"

"Oh please, why wouldn't I like him?" Chandan was floating on air. Then she remembered, "What about you? Aren't you going to get married?"

"Not immediately. I have much to study."

"Arre, won't your Baapu force you to marry?" Fateema was thrown back to a past, a house and Aslam. She had not told Chandan that story.

"Baapu would never force me to do anything."

"Great. You must look for one yourself then, a film hero!"

It was so strange that Chandan did not seem to mind her lack of choice. She was blithely happy. Fateema had not given marriage a thought. She didn't know what was in store for her.

We need to change with the times, Anwar had said. He had been living in Gujarat for three years, so his Urdu was mixed with some Gujarati now. Kareem had followed his advice and given up his hostel accommodation and moved to a Muslim neighbourhood.

Anwar visited him quite often. It was a working-class area full of squalor, noisy quarrels and mosquitoes. Yet he said, "This is fine."

"It'll be good once Fateema gets her B.A.," he said.

"Good from what point of view? An educated khavind, husband?"

"Forget khavind, think of khuda. We need educated women now: Fateema, for a start."

Ten

Fateema climbed the college steps. She saw Chandan and her cousins approaching from the opposite direction. Chandan's face was alight.

"Where are you off to, Chandan? We have an English literature class now."

Chandan and her cousins giggled.

"Fatee, Fatee when will you change?" Chandan's cousin Priya said. They knew Fateema from the many vacations the girls had spent at Chandan's house. Fateema couldn't fathom what exactly was supposed to change. Priya threw light on the subject.

"Learn to relax, girl. Enjoy yourself! You're in college now."

"What's going on though? Where are you people going?"

"We are going home. We came to college to invite some special friends."

"Invite them for what?"

"Chandan's wedding. Here is your kankotri." Priya gave Fateema a wedding card designed with a red bandhni print and a tiny embroidered image of Ganesh on the top. Fateema opened the card and noticed that the groom was 'Surendra Shah' from London.

She looked up to see Chandan's face filled with such joy!

"See your tapasya has borne fruit: you really are off to London!"

The three women left, amidst gaiety and laughter. Fateema stood rooted to the steps long after they had gone. She was happy for Chandan – her friend from the first day of school, the friend who fed her golpapdi during school breaks. Fateema remembered a teary-eyed Chandan when she had goofed up with English spelling. All this and more flashed before her eyes.

"May Allah be with you."

Fateema felt a twinge of regret that Chandan had not made the most of the chance to educate herself. She could have waited a year at least. Never mind, she thought, life had opened up other treasures for her.

All the best, Chandan.

"What is it? Whose wedding do you want to go to?" Kareem asked, somewhat testily. Fateema paled. In four years Kareem had changed beyond recognition.

During her visit to Ba-Baapu (oops, Ammijaan-Abbajaan), Ba had remarked, "He's become a city boy. I told him to go to his old school and pay respects to his teachers, but he didn't budge. He went to see Jamaal, but wouldn't bring him back. Says Jamaal is settled there."

Fateema's elementary knowledge of biology had familiarized her with hormonal changes. That's what she attributed the changes in Kareem to. At least, for now.

However, the way he'd just spoken to her was infuriating. Fateema raised her voice, "Arre, this is Chandan's wedding we are talking about."

"Who is Chandan?" A quiet onlooker so far, Anwar asked.

"She is my friend, almost a sister. We studied together. She even…" Fateema couldn't bring herself to complete the sentence. It wasn't appropriate to mention different kinds of help that Chandan had extended. "Kareem knows how close we are."

"So I don't see what the problem is," said Anwar.

No answer from Kareem.

"All right, I am asking you to go. By the way, you must also go with Kareem and get yourself something special to wear at the wedding. You might as well deck up if you have to go to the wedding. Right, Kareem?"

Kareem smiled somewhat reluctantly.

On their way out, Anwar chided him, "Why are you doing this? We will need not one but many Fateemas. They are our frontline. Let them mix with the public, and let the public trust them. Do you follow?"

Kareem followed but that did nothing to assuage the flames of resentment. He had been dreaming of an Islamic society and the elimination of corrupt, blasphemous Western practices of wearing pants and tops, drinking, partying…

Sitting in the crowd, dressed in a pink zari shalwar kameez, Fateema watched the rituals of Chandan's wedding with great interest.

"You must find all this quite different, no?" An NRI Gujarati woman from London asked her.

"Oh yes, different but interesting. Ultimately, we must all prepare to live in a more multiracial and multi-religious society."

The Gujarati woman was merely making small talk. Her curiousity had been piqued on hearing the name 'Fateema'. The poor woman had not bargained for such eloquence and a level of English that surprised even Fateema herself. Fateema had had such thoughts earlier, but they were not clearly articulated views.

As she lay in bed that night, she heard herself in her sleep.

"When Allah asked the Prophet to create the Koran, Judaism and Christianity were already established religions. Moses, Ezekiel, David and Jesus are considered messiahs by Islam. The root of all three religions is a common ancestor – Abraham."

Fateema was jolted into wakefulness. Why was she speaking as though addressing an audience? Who was she talking to? Her speech on Islam was still a week away. Go back to sleep, Fateema, she told herself.

✳

Chandan's wedding had stirred up some headiness, however briefly. A month or two later, Komal first entered Fateema's room, then her life. She brought with herself an ebullience and fearless joy.

"You are Fateema, right? Rector Madam described you perfectly to the last detail. I am Komal, your roommate."

Fateema unlocked the door to her – now their – room. Komal didn't waste a moment and clicked open her suitcases one by one. No cupboards, no tables in sight. She shut them immediately.

"Hmm. I see. We'll have to live in and out of suitcases." Fateema missed her sarcasm.

Knowing Komal was like being thrown into a carnival of colours and youthful emotions.

'*Khullam-khulla pyaar karenge hum dono,*' played softly on the cassette player Komal had brought with her: We will love, openly and fearlessly. Fateema wondered if the open and fearless voice would reach Manuben's ears. But Komal was far from worried.

Komal came and slept next to Fateema, their bodies touching each other. Fateema felt a tremor run through her.

Oblivious, Komal hummed along with the songs. Then she switched the player off.

"Why are you so nervous? Haven't you ever heard passionate filmy songs, Fateema?"

No answer.

"Where did you grow up then?"

"A tiny village."

A gentle smile on Komal's face.

"Your parents must be quite strict, nah? Girls shouldn't do this, girls shouldn't do that kind of people, right?"

"Somewhat."

Komal pressed Fateema's hand with understanding, "Poor you."

"Why do you use so much English?"

"Because I studied in Mother Mary Convent."

Fateema felt an acute desire to speak English like that.

As time went by, Komal became more open and expressive. Fateema was jolted into a world new to her. Love songs of all kinds, blatant, risqué, coquettish, whatnot, filled the room -- from 'Yaad Kiya Dil Ne' to 'Mehndi Laga Ke' to invitations of kissing in 'Chumma Chumma.' The song 'Ik Ladki Ko Dekha' moved Fateema deeply. She replayed it several times, much to Komal's puzzlement.

"What is so special about this one?"

"See how sacred he thinks beauty is, *jaisa mandir mein koi jalta diya*, 'like a lamp in a temple.' Just listen to it, such poetry!" Fateema waxed eloquent in a mixture of Hindi, English and Gujarati to make herself comprehensible to Komal.

Komal had different tastes, however.

When girls hadn't arrived by 7pm, Manuben would wait at the entrance to 'welcome' them back and tick them off.

Girls like Komal had grown up on a steamy diet of films and fiction. Manuben's discipline had little effect on them.

One night, Fateema heard someone whisper, "Are you awake?"

"Hmm. Tell me."

"No, forget it." Komal turned over. But once again, "You know there are two guys who wait right outside our college."

"Komal, keep away from trouble."

"Arre, what is life without some spice or trouble, eh? Fateema, do you know why love happens?"

"No." Fateema found herself illiterate. It can't be the way they describe it in novels. "How do you know when someone loves you?"

"Oh, that's not difficult."

"But how? Through love letters?"

Komal found Fateema's naivete endearing. Their voices were soft and barely audible. In the quiet dark, these were illuminating lessons.

"You know, even in a group of ten to fifteen people, you can pick up on signals."

"But how?"

"*Ankho hi ankho mein…* the eyes do it."

One day, Komal had apparently received a 'signal.'

"I told you, remember, about those two guys? One of them said to me today, 'Miss, why are you walking in such scorching heat? I can give you a ride.'"

Komal sat by Fateema on her bed and told her. Fateema had also received a signal today: Manuben had informed her that she would not be entitled to hostel accommodation from next year.

Where would she go? She had been to Kareem's room just once. It was unbearably dirty and noisy, and reeked of non-vegetarian food. Fateema had got used to the cleanliness and quiet of the hostel. Manuben saw a shadow of anxiety pass over Fateema's face.

"Why are you so anxious? In any case, your brother will be marrying you off soon. For all you know, your father must be already looking for a groom. This is what happens in your quam."

"No, no, I want to do an MA."

Fateema left to go to her room. This tucked-in-a-corner unventilated room was hers. She was half-listening to Komal.

"Don't be a fool. You can't just take a two-wheeler ride like that from a complete stranger," she warned Komal, like she would her younger siblings.

Life went on quite uneventfully in the following weeks and months. Komal would dress well and go to college. She would also pay respects to the two pictures of Ganesh and Krishna next to her bed. She said to Fateema once: "Feel free to put up pictures of your gods as well."

"Our religion doesn't allow idol worship."

Fateema showed her the English translation of the Koran.

"Here, read this."

He is the God.

God, the Eternal, the uncaused cause and all being.

He begets not, and neither is he begotten, and there is nothing that could be compared to him.

Komal was embarrassed. "I'm sorry, I know so little about your religion."

As a student of History and Social Sciences, Fateema knew the importance of dialogue. She was not offended.

There were articles to be written for the college magazine and assignments to be submitted. She and Komal had fewer conversations. Fateema was also busy preparing for a college seminar on Islam. She often spotted Komal and a man talking to each other outside the college. Who was that?

Well, whatever. She seems to be enjoying herself. It's her final year as well. And it's not my business, anyway. And yet we are connected, even if she's not my responsibility. Some timely advice may be a good idea.

For now, Fateema needed to focus on her studies, get a good grade. Far away, the horizon shimmered with light. The rising sun had spread its rays, touching Fateema as well – an education, great job, and a house for her and her parents, here, in this city. A house with a view.

Kareem had indeed got their village house repaired. Even Aalamchacha's house. He had proudly mentioned that their lane now goes by the name of Maajidbhaivada. But Fateema wanted her own house, however small, and with a balcony.

Such fantasies distracted her from her studies, so she would pack and seal them, and return to the present: first, grades.

It was tiring. Fateema would study during the night as well. Lights in many of the rooms stayed on past midnight these days. Like her, other girls were also busy studying.

One night, Fateema fell asleep with the lights on and a book in her hand. She dreamt of a man standing next to her bed. He was studying her face by torchlight. She wanted to scream, but fear choked her.

It was not a dream.

Eleven

Fateema kept her eyes shut, as if to block out the stranger looming over her. This has to be a nightmare, a result of the strange conversations that Komal had been having with her. But Fateema also knew that she was awake and this was real. He aimed the torch once again at her face. Fateema opened her eyes. She pushed him away, opened her mouth to scream...

"Fateema, it's me."

She recognized the voice. *Komal?*

"Sh... shh... speak softly, that wretched woman will wake up."

Fateema got off the bed. She went and drew the curtains to allow the compound light in. She turned to look at Komal and found her dressed in a shirt and trousers, a cap on her head.

"What's going on? Why are you dressed like this?" Fateema tried keeping her voice low, somewhat unsuccessfully.

"*Pyaar hua ikraar hua...*" Komal hummed gaily. "Listen, I'll be back in a while, make sure that woman doesn't come to know anything."

Komal went and effortlessly removed the net drawn across the windows. She jumped over the windowsill – and was gone. Fateema watched all this, wonderstruck.

How did the net come off so miraculously? Who had

ripped it? Fateema was tempted to inform the matron, but on second thought she decided it was better to deal with Komal directly.

She was wide awake now. Komal came back in an hour. The following week was much too hectic to find the time to talk to Komal. They slept under the same roof, but Komal would turn on her side and promptly go to sleep.

On her way out of the college building, Fateema spotted Anwar, standing on his own. Kareem was not with him. She had met Anwar many times. He was as familiar as the field beyond the house and village, and the man who walked towards that field every day. But on a rain-drenched morning when mottled clouds scurry back and forth and a chirping bird paints a streak across the sky, the familiar assumes newness of the kind Fateema experienced on seeing Anwar that day. He was tall and fair with a well-built body. Why hadn't she noticed that before? Other men on the streets paled in comparison.

He walked towards her. "Fateema."

"Hello."

"Salaam Alekum."

"Oh… Alekum Salaam."

"I came to tell you that Kareem has a high fever."

"Fever?"

"I could have phoned you at the hostel, but then I thought you might want to see him and I could take you there."

"Yes, of course."

Anwar waved for an auto, and explained the directions to the driver. Fateema got in the auto, while Anwar followed her on his bike.

Fateema was disconcerted by the news. How high was Kareem's temperature? As high as Saira's? Allah, be with him.

The auto threaded its way into an overcrowded mohalla. Anwar paid the fare. The two of them walked briskly towards Anwar's single room or 'kholi'.

Amazing, Fateema thought to herself: Kareem left a nice and clean hostel room to live in this hole? She had not seen the boys' hostels at close quarters, but Kareem had told her that the rooms were good.

A shudder ran through her as she realized that in a year's time she might well be looking at a place like this. Anwar had walked ahead of her. He waited for her at Kareem's doorstep. They entered the house together and found Kareem asleep on a single cot.

Fateema felt his forehead. She immediately looked around the room. She found a kettle which she filled up with water. There were no cloth strips obviously. Fateema dipped one end of her dupatta into cold water and put it on Kareem's forehead.

"We consulted the doctor. He advised a blood test."

"How long has he been running this fever? You should have told me. I would have come." There was a catch in her voice.

"Oh no, that wasn't necessary. It shot up only today. Don't worry, I *am* taking care of him."

Anwar covered Kareem up with a thick shawl. Fateema watched him, her eyes filled with gratitude. The medicine brought Kareem's temperature down.

Anwar was ready to leave. Fateema said, "Thank you."

"You don't have to thank me, but if you must, say 'shukriya.' Khuda Hafiz."

"Khuda Hafiz."

She watched Anwar leave.

Kareem's illness continued for several more days. Fateema

had to seek Manuben's permission to come late every day. One day Manuben asked her, "What's going on Fateema? What does the doctor have to say about Kareem's fever?"

"That's the problem, Manuben. The blood test does not show temperature."

"How's that possible?"

"Anwar mentioned this. He's the one overseeing the treatment. We are thinking of admitting him to a hospital."

"Fateema, get a blood test done when the temperature is very high. That's how malaria is detected, they say. The same thing happened to my father as well. The doctors kept saying it was flu, but it turned out to be something else."

"Thanks, I'll tell Anwar that."

Next time, when Kareem had a raging temperature, Anwar got a laboratory technician over for a blood sample. Kareem was diagnosed with malaria.

Two more weeks went by. Kareem slowly recovered and regained his strength.

Meanwhile Fateema continued to vigorously prepare for her forthcoming examination. She expected to be in the top rank.

Anwar's face would occasionally float in front of Fateema's eyes while she was reading. These were glimmerings of new emotions. What was happening to her?

How did Anwar 'fit' into the atmosphere she saw around Kareem's house? He was sophisticated, so different from everything and everyone. Was she falling in love with Anwar? But when had she, as Komal put it, received *signals* from Anwar?

It was two in the afternoon. Some girls were busy studying in the library, a couple had put their heads on the table and dozed off. Fateema was lost in the accounts of

Mahmud Ghazni's raids on the Somnath temple. A dead and boring subject for most students, History came alive for Fateema. Accompanied by a colossal army, as he cut though the mountains, traversed a desert to invade a temple in an unknown land, Mahmud must have been an indubitably impressive warrior. But who was he?

Fateema opened a reference book by a British historian who summed up Mahmud Ghazni as an 'invader' in the Indian context. *What must my country have gone through, when one after another, plunderers came and looted, killed thousands of helpless people, took away women and children as slaves?*

Fateema's history of medieval India had several and contradictory views on Mahmud Ghazni. Was he interested in gold, or political sovereignty, or the dissemination of Islam? Did he harbour hatred towards idolatry – hence Somnath – or was he on a path of personal ambition? History has diverse narratives on this episode. What was clear though, Fateema rued, was that if she, as a dispossessed woman, were to be taken away along with Ba and others and their families were killed while trying to rescue them, it would be unforgivable. Was there no protest against this violence in Ghazni's own society? Was he supported, incited or discouraged by his fellow Muslims? Fateema was agitated, scorched by the heat of the summer that had made its way into the library.

She put away the books. It should be possible to interpret history without making it into a bone of contention. Invasions of this nature have always happened in India. Occasionally both the rulers as well as the invaders were Muslims. Tamerlane had slaughtered ministers of the Tuglaq dynasty, for instance. What was his name? Oh yes, Mubarak Khan. The fact was that violence and war were products of a medieval mind. This was as true of South Asia as of European nations. To wage a war and kill people was considered not just normal but also necessary. *Are we any different today?* Fateema asked herself if she would be able to express what she had been thinking. *Fateema ke naam par fatwa,* she thought with amusement.

It was evening by the time Fateema left the library. She began a gentle and leisurely walk towards the hostel. The street buzzed with life—food, jokes, conversations, vehicles and pedestrians. After a day of reading, Fateema enjoyed the mindless buzz around her.

Her feet stilled as she turned a corner. A two-wheeler whizzed past. Was that Komal? But who was the one driving? Only Komal could have answered that question, but she had vanished into thin air.

Fateema reached the hostel, and found Komal on her bed, reading. Was Fateema hallucinating then? Komal came up to her, held her hand and said:

"Such strangers living under the same roof!"

*

It was the same house, and yet it looked so very different inside and outside.

The mud-baked floor on which Fateema and her three siblings played and rolled about was now plastered with cement. The walls were also cemented. Kareem had had the house painted green. Baapu's body lay on the cement floor. His face showed no sign of pain.

"He has gone away peacefully. See how calm he looks," a doctor remarked.

Baapu must have been ill for a while but he had not wanted to tell anyone, Allah's man that he was. He was on his way to pray, and ended up in Allah's refuge. Wrapped in a black dupatta, Ba was praying, her hands raised to the sky. Relatives from in and around the village and other members of the quam had arrived as soon as they heard the news.

Kareem and Anwar ran errands and made preparations. Anwar had brought Jamaal with him. Fateema watched Jamaal in disbelief. This is Jamaaliyo – this six-foot tall man in a skull cap, with a short beard and spectacles with black frames! Arre, when did he grow up so much? Jamaal came up to Fateema and hugged her. Then resting his head in Ba's lap, he wept and wept. Ba, Fateema, Kareem, Jamaal – Maajidbhai's loved ones – clung to his body and wept. Aayats from the Koran were read out.

Ba, who had braved torrential rains and floods, was a pool of tears today. Fateema's father lay hidden behind a shroud. She said to him, "Baapu, how much you suffered for us. Your dream to see us as equal to the rest will be fulfilled. I will never forget that."

"Baapu shouldn't have wasted himself in this stupid little village. Had he come to the other place, Rajab Ali would have made him prosperous." Jamaal's voice was bitter.

Fateema quickly turned her head. "What did you say?"

"What is there to say? If only these people had listened to me. Look at me now. You know Fatee, I drive Rajab Ali's imported car. I have also learned to repair vehicles. Hopefully I will also have my own transport business. This poor man went around cycling all day and just copped it."

"Shut up," Fateema hissed.

"Shhh," Moulviji motioned everyone to be quiet. It was time to take the body for burial.

"*Ammijaan ko sambhalo.*" Anwar asked Fateema to take care of Ba.

Fateema went and sat next to her.

"Don't lose heart, Ba, we are there to look after you. Baapu was tired, so Allah called him over."

Ba calmed down a bit. "Child, you don't worry about me. In fact I am worried about Jamaal."

Ba was Ba after all. Without exchanging a word with Jamaal, she had been able to suss him out. What could Fateema add?

Jamaal had had a taste of luxury and indulgence, away from the scarcities of his childhood, and away from the backbreaking work and low returns. After dealing with shiny, big cars and being privy to business deals worth large sums of money, Jamaal was bound to dismiss a life of poverty.

"Ba, Jamaal can draw water out of rocks, you shouldn't worry about him."

"That's what bothers me."

Anwar left and mattresses were laid out on the floor for the siblings to sleep in a Baapu-less house. It was a night just like when Saira died – they were all awake.

Kareem left the next morning, leaving behind for Ba a thick wad of notes. "Anwarbhai left this," he said to Fateema. Jamaal left that afternoon. Fateema stayed back.

Twelve

A fragile house, but its inhabitants had been strong, like pillars. *That's what turned me into Dr. Fateema rather than just Fateema.* How would Ba and Baapu have reacted to hearing her addressed as 'Daaktar Fateema?' Arre, Ba would giggle, "Will you give injiktion to people, that kind of daaktar?" Baapu would stroke his beard and wisely say, "She'll definitely give it to someone." Momentarily the absence of Jamaal, Kareem and Saira would be forgotten and a wave of happiness would pass through the house.

What kind of dream was this? Fateema was jolted out of her sleep. It was seven in the morning. She had better hurry or else there'll be a long queue at the bathroom. Worse than waiting in the queue was the prospect of a wet and dirty bathroom. Dr Fateema was now a teacher in senior college. She also taught graduate students. Fateema raised her hands to the sky to pray. Packing up her fantasies in a pile of clothes, she left to shower. It was her immediate future that she should be thinking about.

"Please sit, Madhubhai has not arrived yet."

"He gave me an appointment for ten."

"Ben, many people visit him at home, so he may be running late. Don't worry."

The peon offered her a chair.

Fateema opened her purse to take a handkerchief out and

wipe her face. Along with the hanky came a packet of bindis. "Oh, I should have put a bindi on, and simply mentioned it if the matter came up." The momentary temptation gave way to, "How long can a house founded on untruth last?" She put the bindi packet back into the purse.

A large white car pulled up beyond the barbed wire that surrounded the complex. A man dressed in white got down. He went to the makeshift office near the construction site.

Hesitant at first, Fateema quickly followed him, "Mr. Kapadia?"

"Yes? Please take a seat."

"The apartments in this complex..."

"Hmm, there are a couple left."

"Can I see the plans please? I'm looking for a one-bedroom apartment."

"What did you say? Oh yes, the plans. I suggest you leave your card with us. I will let you know what is available once my partner is back." With this, he buried his head in some papers. The peon placed some tea on the table.

"I don't have a card but I don't mind swinging by again. Just tell me when I should come. You gave me an appointment for ten today, so I thought..."

He looked up. "Ben, we are comfortable with a gents-to-gents deal. What is there to discuss with womenfolk, hanh? It's the men who do business, right? Send your man."

Three men entered the room. Mr. Kapadia stood up with alacrity to welcome them. They took no notice of Fateema.

"Gents-to-gents, of course." Fateema left the room, bitter.

She saw the peon waiting outside.

"The foundations of the building are not yet laid, so tell me, how come all the apartments are sold already?"

"Ben, how would I know what goes on inside that room? But if you don't quote me, let me tell you that I heard Kapadia Saheb mention to somebody on the phone that he did not have all clearances yet. So Ben, you better be careful, people like you and I buy things with our lives' savings. You don't want to get stuck."

Here she was, scared of sticking a bindi on her forehead, whereas Mr. Kapadia was ready to erect a building without permission. Chaalo, she said to her two-wheeler, time to get back.

It was Niruben who had given her this address and reference, and mentioned that Kapadia was a good builder. Fateema was thrilled. A little bedroom, a living room and a tiny kitchen. Allah, was that too much to ask? What sacrifices do you want me to make? Chiding herself for such sacrilege, she quickly murmured, Inshallah. Three days later, Fateema found herself at Mr. Kapadia's office again. Her told her, very regretfully, that all the apartments had been sold.

"I know, I know you did come, but I'm so sorry. I will let you know if something turns up. After all our job is to sell, Ben. Okay, bye."

She mentioned this to Niruben. No comments from her. Not even a mention that Mr. Kapadia's business partner was Niruben's first cousin. Fateema looked despondent. Niruben was saddened to see that.

"Fateemaben, the thing is you are a single woman, so other members in the building may not feel comfortable…." She didn't finish.

"It's all right, Niruben, some other time." It didn't seem right to discuss such details in the faculty room. Fateema was well aware that people listening would make a mountain of a molehill. More importantly, she had consciously taken a decision to stay single and was determined not to be seen as a pitiable object.

Ekla baaimaanas, they say for single women. So that was threatening, was it? A seductress, who lured away the husbands, and frightened the wives? The building must protect its men and wives from the wiles of a single woman, right? Fateema shook with anger and helplessness. *Educated men with rotten thoughts: my illiterate and proud mother is far superior to them.*

Fateema visited Ba during her vacations. This was after Baapu's death. She had six months left to complete her B.A.

She dropped by at the school. It was recess time. The school compound buzzed with noisy activities as students played games like gillidanda, saattaali and cricket. Fateema stood watching. Across the compound still stood the tree under which she and Chandan exchanged lunch, Fateema's chana and Chandan's golpapdi. She saw some girls laughing and chatting under the same tree.

Chandan now teaches Gujarati and Hindi every weekend at a school in London. She wrote to Fateema almost a year after her marriage and said, "Each time I enter a classroom I think of you, Fatee. After all, I am able to teach others only because you taught me."

Fateema went to the office upstairs to meet Gaekwad Sir. He ordered tea.

"What do you plan to do after your B.A.?"

"I don't know Sir. At the moment, I can't think beyond my B.A."

"That, of course, will be over and done with. But do remember that the gates of this school are always open for you. You can walk in anytime and teach here. I can make arrangements for you take a Bachelors in Education."

"A B.Ed?"

"It's mandatory now for all school teachers."

Fateema had not given this a thought. Her silence did not escape Gaekwad Sir's notice.

"There's no pressure. Cities offer many opportunities for growth, I can understand that. But I had a different perspective."

"Such as?"

"You know, Fateema, how far behind we are with women's education, generally speaking. Muslim parents are particularly reluctant to send their daughters to school. A teacher like you, who is self-reliant, independent and fearless, and also supports an old mother, would be a great role model for other girls."

"I –"

"I would love to see you sit in my chair." He smiled and made light of the matter. Both of them knew that she had not said yes.

On her way out, Fateema stood watching the school compound again. She wanted to reach up to the sky and kiss it. She may not have agreed to take up the offer, but she was certainly flattered and honoured to be considered eligible for the highest position in the school. This school had turned a girl called Fatee who squashed mud to make walls, made fuel out of cowdung, gave tuitions for two measly laddus into Fateema, B.A. She had been liberated from the toil of her mother's life. The fence of poverty and pity had been crossed.

"So what did your Master say?" Ba had made two cups of tea. She was cooling her heels in the verandah, now tiled with cement. She had had a cataract operation and now wore thick glasses. She still had some stitching and sewing jobs. When Fateema made her give that up, she said, "My hands begin to bite me when they have nothing to do." Fateema let the matter rest.

"They are offering me a job here."

"Oh yes? How good that is. We can catch hold of Jamaaliyo as well and all live together. He has not surfaced since Baapu's death."

Fateema did not want to extend the conversation about Jamaal. Kareem had told her that Jamaal had quit being Rajab Ali's driver and left the village. He was now in Bombay. Ba did not know that.

"I don't know if I should take up the offer."

"Why not?"

"Ba, I don't really feel like working as yet. I want to study further."

"Even more? You've studied so much already."

"There's a lot left, Ba. I want to do an M.A. for two years, that will give me a much better job."

Ba understood the language of jobs better than education or research.

"You know I'd get paid to study. It's called a scholarship. But there would be two years more to go."

"Two years it is then. Finish it up. We are hardly starving here."

Ba and her colloquialisms! She had agreed with such simplicity that a huge cloud lifted off Fateema's mind.

"Really, Ba? You don't mind?"

"Did I ever?"

Fateema stopped her from going into the kitchen to return the empty cups. She took them instead. Then holding Ba's hand in her own, she said, "Ba, thank you."

"See? I've again forgotten what to say in return. I know you had taught me something. Consider it said."

Fateema laughed.

"When someone says 'thank you,' you are expected to say 'my pleasure'."

She took Ba in her arms, allowing a tear to roll down her cheek. She said to herself, *Thanking you is not enough Ba. I will take you with me to a little house on the third or fourth floor. Bas, just a few more years.*

The mother and daughter talked late into the night. Fateema narrated hostel stories to her, a novel matter for Ba who listened with rapt attention. Every now and then she was impressed by Manuben, "Oh ho, so much responsibility, how many girls she looks after and their fees and everything, na?"

Ba was upset to hear about Kareem's illness. "Shouldn't you have called me?"

Fateema avoided telling her about Kareem's house or kholi in a dirt-filled basti. She also avoided telling her much about Komal. But she did relate to her Manuben's timely advice regarding malaria and how that helped Kareem recover.

Moved, Ba said, "See that's Allah's people for you. Otherwise why would she do it, she doesn't even know me? That's what being human is about."

Ba joined Fateema to see her off at the bus station. Fateema was silent lest she break down. She sat by the window in the bus while Ba stood nearby, saying, "Don't worry about me, just take care of Kareem. He must be working so hard to send me money all the time." Ba wiped the tears from her eyes.

The bus conductor rang the bell for departure.

"Fatee, say thank you to Kareem on my behalf and –"

Before Ba could finish, the bus began to move. Ba waved, "And also tell him khuda hafiz."

The bus set off in the direction of Fateema's independent

existence. Ba went in the direction of her home, a sob caught in her throat.

＊

Ekla baimaanas, single woman, they said. Fateema felt very angry, without knowing how to vent her anger.

It's not Niruben's fault. It's a curse: the curse of being a woman.

Fateema had read an autobiography by an Iranian woman who wanted to go to England to study. This was around the time of World War II. It was not common practice to travel alone. Before she embarked upon her voyage, her brother asked her to go to a restaurant across the road and have a meal.

"What? Go to eat alone?"

"If you wish to study and survive alone, you must also get used to travelling and eating alone."

The Iranian woman went to the restaurant, and sat alone among unknown men. She learnt an important lesson that day – a lesson that Fateema, too, would also have to learn. She would be regarded with suspicion.

Fateema entered the hostel room and put her tiny suitcase in a corner. She sat on the bed, staring vacantly at the wall. It had cracks, and it looked darker as well. She had noticed this before. Fateema sat there wondering how to collect dispersed memories and frame them.

She pushed herself to get up and drink some water. Ba used to insist on giving her a water bottle during every visit. She had forgotten this time. Fateema looked at the earthen pot in the corner. Did Komal rinse it, or simply refill it? She took the matka, cleaned it and filled it up with cold water from the water cooler.

She came back and once again sat on the bed. Someone knocked. It was Manuben. She entered the room, and put an arm around Fateema.

"Did you just come? Had tea?"

"No."

"Come, I'll order tea in my office." Fateema followed Manuben to her office. Kantaben placed two cups of tea on the table. Manuben took out a packet of biscuits from the drawer and offered them to Fateema.

"Eat this, Ben, you must be tired. And cheer up now."

Manuben's phone rang. She picked up the receiver and listened to something that made her frown. She handed the receiver to Fateema.

"Hello?"

"Hello Fatee? This is Jamaal. I am in Bombay doing business here."

"I know. Kareem told me. Stay with Ba, Jamaal, and finish your education."

"Fatee, you are just…" Jamaal hung up.

Thirteen

Fateema put the receiver back on the cradle. She looked pensive. Manuben stopped sipping her tea. "What happened, Fateema? Anything serious?"

"No, that was my younger brother. He has gone away to Bombay to do business."

"Smart fellow he is. He will manage well by himself. You don't worry about him. Chalo, drink your tea."

Fateema took a deep breath, almost readied herself for life's pleasant, nasty and shocking surprises every day.

The tea ritual ended. Something arrived by post – a very large packet with envelopes as well as postcards. It was placed on Manuben's table.

"Applications for hostel admission next year. I get this many every single day."

"Manuben, I will prepare a data-sheet for you, with individual sections on names, age, college, parents' income etc. It will be like a ready reckoner for you."

"Arre, would you really do that? That will make it so easy for me. Thanks, Fateema." Manuben held her hand.

"My pleasure." Fateema stood up to leave. So did Manuben.

"You are a strong girl, Ben. You will fulfil the dreams your father had for you."

Then putting an arm around Fateema, she continued, "A

generation passes away, and another one takes its place, that's life. Cry when you must, but also remember the future ahead of you."

Thinking that she might have said too much, Manuben went back to her table.

Inshallah, Fateema said to herself.

Everyday life – the hostel, her studies, the exams, the library – rolled over and over like a giant wheel and the past once again began to fade to a distant memory. This has happened before, has it not? When she left home to come to the city she left behind Ba, Baapu, school; it had all been gently wiped away. Perhaps all memories merge like cells into the bloodstream where they keep the heart beating and weightlessly carry the past.

Komal had been with Fateema ever since she returned from the village. She didn't know how to console her friend, but she tried drawing her into conversation about college.

"Fateema, look who's here to meet you!" Komal stood outside the college waiting for Fateema. "How does he know me? He's asking me when you'll come out, when your lectures are over." Komal pointed to Anwar standing next to his two-wheeler under a tree across the road.

"That's Anwar, Kareembhai's friend. He's probably brought a message from Kareembhai."

Fateema walked up to Anwar with Komal tagging along behind.

"Salaam Alekum." Anwar did the aadaabs.

"Alekum Salaam."

"How is Ammijaan?"

"She's fine. Chachi has been looking after her. In any case, Ba is strong."

"*Emaj hona chahiye,*" he said in a mix of Gujarati and Urdu.

"That's how it should be. Sorry, my Gujarati's not perfect yet. Anyway, I came to tell you that Kareembhai is out of town. He'll be back in a day or two."

"Out of town? But where?"

"He had some work. He'll be back soon, as I said."

"What about his studies? This is his final year after all."

"Fateemaji, Kareembhai is quite capable of looking after himself. Stop worrying about him."

Komal chimed in, "Fateemaji is a compulsive worrier. She's unhappy if she has nothing to worry about."

Anwar and Fateema laughed.

"*Aapki pehchaan?*" Anwar asked Komal.

"I am Komal, Fateema's friend and roommate." Holding Fateema's hand, Komal said to Anwar, "Let's make Fateema's life lighter, what do you say?"

"Absolutely, it's necessary to have change. Generally men and women don't meet openly in our community, but since you are around…"

"So, a film tomorrow?" Komal wasted no time.

"*Ekdum* first class."

"Arre, wait I…" Brushing aside Fateema's predictable objection, Komal immediately said, "I will take Manuben's permission."

"So, we'll meet tomorrow at 4 pm at the cinema hall." Komal gave parting instructions.

On the way back, as she and Komal headed towards the hostel, Fateema noticed that Komal, who had been raised on a diet of Mills and Boon romances, couldn't contain her excitement about a romantic film the following day.

The next day, they found Anwar waiting outside the cinema hall, but he wasn't alone. Anwar introduced his friend Mazhar – an engineering student. The two of them had already bought the tickets. Fateema felt quite uncomfortable. The fact that she was watching a film with Kareem's friends while Kareem himself was absent bothered her. Kareem could have at least left a message – but it was too late to back out. Anwar and Mazhar left to go to the paan shop. Fateema seized the opportunity and ticked Komal off. "Next time, don't include me in your plans."

"Fatee, Fatee," Komal humoured her. "Just look at us, young and merry, and the lovely weather, and such good company!"

"Komal, stop spouting filmy dialogues, and get your feet back on the ground."

"Now that you are here, just enjoy yourself, will you? Look, the guys are coming back. Have you met this Mazhar fellow before?"

"No."

"Such a sweet face, seriously! I have to admit that your brother's friends are all good looking."

The two men joined them and together they went inside the cinema hall. Same old story, same old dialogues and same faces, but Komal was enchanted.

That night, she slid into Fateema's bed. Gently, "Fatee, can you hear me?"

"Shh."

"Stop shushing me, yaar." Komal pressed Fateema's hand to her own cheek. "What a love story that was! Did you like it?"

In the hollow darkness of the room, lit only by the intermittent shards of a street light shining through the branches of the tree outside, Komal's voice seemed to come from a distance like an echo. She seemed to say a lot, but what stuck out with greatest clarity to Fateema's straining ears was the word 'love.'

Fateema gently removed Komal's hand from her body. With her eyes filled with dreams and fantasies, Komal seemed oblivious to the room, or the fact that Fateema was shining a torch on her face.

"Komal, go to bed please."

"No, let me stay Fatee… oh God, doesn't anything happen to you?"

"Komal, please."

"Fateema, please. I am fully awake, I can't sleep now, I need…"

Komal left the rest unspoken.

"Just splash some water on your face, and think of a God you believe in, and you'll be able to sleep."

"How can you be so passionless? Don't you have fantasies of a man, some professor, some boyfriend?"

Something rattled in the corridor outside. Komal immediately left to sleep in her own bed. The rattling died down. Since the room was in the basement, rats scurried between the compound and the corridor.

"There's nothing to feel scared about, silly," Komal said.

"Just as well. Now go to sleep quietly."

"Same old dialogues again," Komal muttered. "Once you fall in love, you'll know what I'm talking about."

Struck by a sudden thought, Komal asked, "Arre tell me, why haven't you fallen in love with Anwar?"

Fateema's heart raced. She didn't answer. Komal went to sleep. Her question had led to many others. Looking for answers, Fateema, too, slipped into slumber.

Fateema's cheek stung. Kareem had slapped her. She was watching a film with other men. Fateema woke up feeling heat on her cheek.

This idiot Komal, she thought.

"Fateema, let's go for a matinee show today."

"There are classes in the morning, in case you've forgotten."

Fateema knew that Komal had not forgotten classes – in fact they served as a good ruse. You don't need Manuben's permission to attend classes.

"Who are you going with?" Fateema asked.

"A friend, rather friends."

"I don't want to come, and you shouldn't go either."

"Arre yaar, you've become a Mini-Manuben."

Fateema was enraged. But it was also funny – she couldn't help but be amused.

The visitors' room had a television now. It had brought to the hostel a profusion of sights and sounds, products and desires, stirring up not only Komal's heart, but that of every other girl in the hostel. They were watching advertisements one night. A woman was pouring tea from a teapot. She handed the cup to a man. Their eyes met, and they smiled.

"What a handsome man," cooed Sanjna, a third-year B.A. student, who had a room on the second floor.

"You should have seen the hero in *Titanic*. A Greek God, I tell you."

"This one looks like Anwar, Fateema's friend," Komal said, pointing to the male model on screen.

All eyes turned towards a flustered Fateema.

"What are you saying, Komal? He's Kareembhai's friend. I don't even know his full name. You just babble."

"Sorry, very sorry." Komal apologized.

"Do show him to us when he's here, never mind if he's related to you or not," one of the girls teased

Everyone laughed.

"Anyway, Manuben will be here any moment to turn off the TV." Fateema left, so did the rest.

A shadowy presence in Fateema's consciousness had taken form now – Anwar. A sweet longing had made its way into her heart, thanks to Komal's company and her own youth. Anwar seemed so genteel and sophisticated, almost a different race. With light eyes, fair skin and well-built body, he looked like someone who lived in the mountains. But he constantly spoke of Islamic life as a refuge. Fateema had disagreements there.

Also, a vital and absorbing part of Fateema's life lay in her books. When she pored over history books, she was miles away, away from hostel, from Komal and even Anwar. She was a traveller then, groping for the present in the alleys of the past. At times such as these, only her body inhabited the library, perspiring under a fan that whirred ineffectually.

Fateema was in the world of Jesus Christ today. Reading and interpreting the rise of Christianity, removing as she went along, the patina of bigotry and disbelief to see history for what it was, how it happened. Fateema noticed legends and facts slip and slide, assuming different names for the same thing. The episode of Noah's Ark in Christianity when Noah saved the life of man and beast, resonated with Vishnu's transformation as a tortoise to save the earth from the flood. A thrill ran through her as she made these discoveries. She decided to read more on the basics of Hinduism. Fateema borrowed some books and was putting them in her bag, when Komal entered.

"Come outside, your brother wants to see you."

Fateema saw Mazhar, Kareem and Anwar standing under a tree outside the library. She hadn't seen Kareem for many days. She had not told him about Jamaal's phone-call – anyway, this was not the time.

"What's going on Fateema? We have been waiting here for half an hour."

"Oh, I must tell you what I read today-" Fateema stopped herself. She noticed that Kareem and Anwar were not interested. Meanwhile, Mazhar and Komal had moved away from the rest. Kareem and Anwar exchanged a look, which did not escape Fateema's notice. She felt a twinge, almost bitter.

Komal waved at Fateema to say bye and left with Mazhar on his two-wheeler.

"Arre, where did these two go?" Fateema asked, realizing soon that it was a dud question.

"Let's go, Fateema." Kareem and Anwar began to walk.

"Where?"

"My place. You will have to wait there until Komal is back, otherwise that draconian rector of yours won't let her in without you." Kareem laughed, so did Anwar.

They reached Kareem's house. Fateema was silent.

Anwar bought some tea and sandwiches along the way. He put them down and said, "This is good. We are back to our safe house. Nobody knows we are here."

"Meaning?" Fateema asked.

"It means that…" Kareem began to explain. Anwar cut in, "Kareem, quiet."

"What does safe house mean?" Fateema asked.

"Just eat for now," Anwar ordered. Fateema did not like his tone but she found his proximity pleasant.

Fourteen

"We are talking of the safety that a solid roof gives to a house," an overanxious Anwar explained. He knew Fateema had taken offence.

Anwar smiled. He had worn a pathani suit that looked quite distinct with colourful embroidery on it. It was not from Gujarat. Where was he from?

"Where do you live?" Fateema asked him

"Well, my house…" He sipped some tea.

"Lucknow. They have a big kothi there," Kareem put in.

"Oh yes? And when did you see it?" she asked, laughing.

"During one of the vacations. Anwar and I are going out for a while, you make some paranthas in the meantime."

"Yes, *bahut achha, theek.*" A confused Anwar spoke in a mixture of Hindi, Gujarati and English.

"Anwarji, since you are from Lucknow you must be a fluent Hindi speaker. Why don't you just speak in Hindi?" Fateema said to him.

Anwar hesitated a little. "Chalo, Kareem." And with this, he rose to leave.

She'd have time to make paranthas later, Fateema thought, and decided to make a start on the books she had brought along. She took them out of her bag. Kareem had changed his clothes, and was about to leave. He was furious.

"What is this you are reading?"

"Arre, these are my study books."

"These are your study books? This idolatory – and these pictures? Throw them away."

"Kareem, stop it. These are not to be thrown away. You have absolutely…"

"Yes, I am religious, and you don't know that there are no Gods but One and no books but One," Kareem's anger shook her.

"Kareem, calm down please. Don't be such a radical. I have not forgotten the namaaz we did with Baapu and Ba and the Urs we visited. That is my religion. But I will not shut the doors of my consciousness as you want me to do, that's not possible. Please." She pushed him away.

"Shut up! Your tongue's wagging too much these days. We intend to advise every family to make its women wear a burkha. You will also have to wear one."

"Kareem, enough now. Let's go," Anwar said.

Fateema watched her brother in a daze. She had known that this was not the Kareem who recited Saraswati prayers in the school compound, but such anger, such change?

"Kareem, pipe down. We don't want to be overheard. A safe house must not make any noises." Anwar's voice was stern.

Anwar looked at Fateema and smiled. "Sorry, Fateemaji, a house means calm, right? A place where people live harmoniously, without squabbles, in that sense a safe house. Kareem, let's go." He pulled Kareem away with him.

Fateema had no enthusiasm left to read. Why had Kareem become so strange? Anwar seemed to be a wise man. He managed to keep Kareem under control. Fateema came out of the house. She saw an open sewer with dirty water, stinking gutters, two women arguing with each other, a cacophony of roosters and goats, and the smell of meat being cooked. She covered her nose and beat a hasty retreat. She had a strong urge to pack up her books and leave. But what was to be done about Komal? How long had she known Mazhar? And how did Anwar know him?

Under a wooden table in a corner she saw boxes containing flour, oil and dal. She put some flour in an aluminium thaali and began making parathas.

Her eyes went up to the clock: ten to six. Hostel! No sign of Komal yet. Manuben will skin her alive. She quickly cleaned up everything. Komal or no Komal, she had to get back to the hostel. Why should she cover up for Komal, why not let her learn a lesson or two? The next moment, Anwar's words came back to her: take Komal with you to the hostel. *He'll be upset, let me do it for him, just once.* Five, ten minutes past, half past six. Fateema continued to wait in anger. Couldn't Anwarjee have bought a nice little house here, after living in a mansion in Lucknow?

She realized what was nagging at her: the source of her discomfort was the environment she was in. Some days ago Niruben had invited her home for her daughter's birthday. Two bedrooms and a little living room, a lovely balcony with a swing and some plants.

That's enough for one or two people. Couldn't she and Kareem buy a house at some point? Or perhaps she and Anwar?

"Fateema?" Someone called, shaking her out of her reverie. Fateema came out of the house. Kareem and Anwar stood there. Kareem held a packet in his hand.

"Here, take this with you."

"What is it?"

"Your identity."

"Kareem, you are the limit! Fateemaji, Kareem felt like seeing you in a burkha. Treat this as his present to you," Anwar said.

Fateema was at a loss for words. Kareem was ordering her, whereas Anwar was giving her a choice: wear it if you like. She took the packet.

Both men were trying to thrust a specific identity upon her. Before she could say anything, a two-wheeler pulled over beside her.

"Fateemaji, hurry up please. I have dropped Komal outside the hostel but she can't go in without you."

Fateema picked up her bag. She kicked the burkha under the bed. Covering her head, she sat behind Kareem, who drove Mazhar's two-wheeler. She joined Komal, who stood a little away from the hostel. The two of them entered the hostel building, with Komal merrily chatting away, making it appear to Manuben at least that the two friends had been together. Fateema felt uncomfortable at such a lie.

Love scenes from the films Komal had been watching shimmered in the dark like fireflies.

"*Mughal-e-Azam* had such a romantic moment Fateema! Prince Saleem strokes Anarkali's cheek with a feather while she is sleeping... so cute."

Komal was gradually and softly sculpting a universe of romance with words.

"Fateema, what a dance there was in *Dil to Pagal Hai* – this poor orphan girl is not able to speak out and say she's in love with somebody else."

Komal's voice caught then and even now.

"Even Mazhar began to cry. He respects me so much." Komal's voice was as light as a feather. Then she fell asleep.

Fateema lay awake staring at the ceiling. She saw shimmering fireflies in the dark.

Anwar is modern and wise. He's not a fanatic like Kareem. He'll be able to understand me. They could live in a small house together.

What did Komal say the other day? Yes, 'signal.' Had she received one from Anwar? *Anwar, I am slow, perhaps I am not able to understand your signals. Why don't I make an overture?*

Oh shut up, Fateema, you have other goals to achieve. A Masters degree, employment, a house into which you can bring Ba and make her sit on a swing in the balcony. But Anwar can also be a part of that, a house will become a home then. Maybe not a palace like Prince Saleem's. But a small house.

*

"Chalo, ready?"

"Yes."

"That's a full-throated yes 'here,' it better be like that 'there.'"

"Consider that done, Anwarbhai, 'there'."

"All right, let's go then. Has everyone arrived?"

"There's only three people."

"Three is enough." With this, Anwar left. Briefcases and books in their hands, Mazhar, Javed and Kareem locked up Kareem's kholi and followed as instructed.

They were dressed in trousers and T-shirts. They left the two-wheeler behind and took off on foot. It was eleven in the morning and the lanes of the basti were full of activity. Despite it being a holiday, traffic was heavier than on other days. All four of them had exited separately and continued to walk separately till they reached the end of the mohalla.

It was the fourth day of the Ganpati festival. The main road beyond the mohalla was abuzz with people in celebration mode. Idols of Ganpati were being carried in trucks, autos and twowheelers for the ritual submersion and cries of 'Ganpati Baapa Morya' filled the air. Crowds followed the vehicles, their clothes and the many festoons creating a medley of colour. Devotional frenzy filled the air.

Anwar watched tight-lipped, while Kareem and Javed looked on, fascinated. A little girl ran up to them, and thrust some saakariya-chana in Kareem's hand saying it was 'prasaad' and ran back, laughing.

"See that? Idolatory," Anwar said with distaste.

"This happens every year, a ten-day festival. The entire town celebrates," Kareem said, putting the prasaad into his mouth.

"Kareem, you sound like a kaafir." Kareem was embarrassed. He had yet to be purified.

"Sorry, Anwarbhai, I didn't mean it like that." Then he added, "We also participate in the celebration, having witnessed it for so many years. It provides jobs for some of our people who make idols, stitch clothes, sell flowers, beat the drums. It is, after all, a festival of joy."

"Anyway, I brought you here so that all of you get trained to blow up the trucks carrying the idols with the bombs hidden under your kurtas. No sign of a full body anywhere, a limb here, a nose there."

"Suicide bombers? Anwarbhai, my mother will die weeping. My sister, my brother..."

"Is it right to kill people like that? Women, children? Is this Allah's command?" Javed asked.

Anwar expected questions like this: he had encountered them before. But he was furious. *Bloody villagers*, he thought to himself, *more afraid of killing, rather than dying. It's Gandhi's doing, reading him has made them useless.* Then he said, "Kareem, Javed, you have not done your homework which is why you consider the enemies of Islam your friends." Anwar had inadvertently spoken loudly, he quickly looked round to see if anyone had heard.

"There's a majlis at noon today. You know where to come, right? The farmhouse. You'll be paid money for your job there."

Kareem and Javed laughed.

"Anwarbhai, what a *khichhdi* you make of Gujarati and Hindi!"

All of them dispersed with different questions in their minds.

Behind a mehndi hedge at the farmhouse stood a Maruti car, the only sign of human presence. Otherwise the place seemed silent and deserted. Sitting behind the closed doors of the farmhouse on cane chairs were Anwar and Haafiz. Anwar spoke to Haafiz with great deference, although Haafiz seemed to be only ten or twelve years older.

"I am training six to seven men here, some of them are science students."

"Your Gujarati is not bad!"

"I make good khichhdi," Anwar laughed.

"How much longer will it take? There are constant inquiries from 'above'."

"Jee. I am working hard. Ammiji is in London, the authorities have become very strict there as well." Anwar sounded disappointed.

"This is our test. Understand? Allah will be with us."

"It's difficult to recruit fidayeen here. The ones from Yemen, Tashkent, Uzbekistan are willing to die for 1000 dollars, but the ones here…"

"What is the problem?"

"The ones here are scared of killing, not of being killed. Reading Gandhi in school has made them bloody kaafirs."

"What, really?"

"Arre, I tried explaining to them, asked them to blow up trucks, and let streams of blood flow."

"And then?"

"Javed says: how can we kill women and children?"

Haafiz thumped his fist on his palm. "That's it, Anwar, what kind of language are you using? You need different imagery, silly, for convincing people. For communicating to the public, you don't need x-rays, but pictures of gold. Don't talk of dying, talk of martyrdom. Just see how I talk to these boys."

Fifteen

A bunch of young men were playing chess at the farmhouse. They glanced expectantly at the door from time to time. Finally it opened. Salaams were exchanged.

"Our guest today – Haafizbhai. He will address you today," Anwar said.

"Salaam *dosto*. Anwar mentioned that you are Allah's soldiers, happy to sacrifice for Allah."

The men exchanged looks. In a calm voice, Haafiz asked, "Do you know about the life of the Prophet? Do you know how Islam was born?"

Switching immediately to pure Gujarati he said, "Are you following me?"

"Arre, you speak Gujarati!" Everyone was pleasantly surprised.

"Of course. I am a Gujarati, so why wouldn't I speak the language? My father migrated to Pakistan from Kutiyana when Pakistan was formed. My mother still speaks Gujarati at home," Haafizbhai said with a smile.

"But…" Anwar did not complete his sentence.

"I am a pure and religious Muslim in Pakistan. I have lived in Kabul, and in Kashmir. People think I am an Afghani or Kashmiri. But remember this, I am Allah's messenger." His voice was arresting. "Islam was born when the Prophet left Mecca to go to Medina. Islam was not born when Allah revealed the Koran to the Prophet, nor even when the Prophet was born. All of you know how the Qureshis tortured the Prophet in Mecca. The Prophet did hijrat from Mecca to Medina. He established the first mosque in Medina. In the following year the Qureshis invaded Mecca with a huge army. This war was waged in the holy month of Ramzan. On the one hand, an army; on the other, a handful of Muslims…"

Haafiz paused for effect. His audience had lapped up every word. He clenched his fist and raised it high, "The Prophet said to Allah, 'Ya Allah, if Muslims die today, there'll be none left to worship you.' With this, the Prophet collapsed. When he gained consciousness he saw that his horse was being drawn by Angel Gibreel. The Muslim soldiers were being helped by angels wearing white turbans.

"Friends, the faithful know since then that Allah will help them through every war. The war continues, my dear men. It is against the Western world, against the infidels, against each and every person who refuses to embrace Islam. Surrender yourself to this jihad, achieve martyrdom! The Prophet has promised you beautiful virgins in heaven. Remember, you may lose a battle but will win a war. Allah ho Akbar…" Haafiz called out.

The young listeners sat with their backs straight, their faces taut and shiny with anger. A current surged through every vein of Kareem's body. Haafiz's words had set fire to a dry log of wood.

"Palestine is ours, Kashmir is ours. Destroy Israel."

Haafiz paused and looking into the young men's eyes, he asked, "Tell me, who is ready to go for training? Javed? Kareem?"

Javed did not respond, instead he looked at Kareem and Anwar. Then he said, "I need some time to think this over."

Anwar distributed pamphlets about jihad.

"Take your time. You don't need to tie a bomb to your body this minute. Kareem has to learn to make bombs first. A jihadi needs an all-rounded education."

Haafiz moved to lighter subjects, and some of the tension dissipated. Everyone left wishing each other 'Khuda Hafiz'. Anwar and Haafiz were the last ones to leave. Anwar complimented Haafiz, "You were just amazing. Who would have thought you could speak Gujarati!"

Kareem was walking away with a surge of energy. No longer a villager, an unemployed Bachelor of Science, he was soldier for Allah – a fidayeen.

She had not informed Kareem about her plans to visit his house. She picked up a broom and dustpan on her way. It was high time his room was cleaned. The poor man was busy studying and attending tuitions. He even managed to send money to Ba every month. This was the least she could do for her brother.

Fateema entered the room armed with an old kurta to use as a duster. While she swept the floor, she noticed the cloth packet containing the burkha lying unopened and untouched under the bed. Fateema decided to make room for it in the old suitcase she spotted. She ran a duster over it and opened it up. Her eyes widened. The suitcase contained a stack of files with 'Haafiz' written on top. Transfixed, Fateema's eyes roved over the material inside the files. Jihadi literature? Was Kareem a jihadi? Her hands trembled.

One of the files contained photographs of famous landmarks, stations and institutions in India.

"Shut that damn thing," Kareem hollered behind her. "What are you doing here?" His voice sounded pitiless.

A frightened Fateema whirled around and looked him in the eye. Sunlight streamed into the room. She had left the door open, and Kareem had appeared without her realising.

Pointing to the files she now held in her hand, Fateema said sternly, "What is this?"

"What is what?"

"What are these files doing here? And why are you collecting this kind of stuff?"

"Here, give them to me. They belong to somebody else," Kareem said evasively.

He shut the suitcase with a bang and kicked it underneath the bed. Fateema chose to remain quiet.

"What are you doing here?"

"Cleaning your place, what else? No wonder you fall sick in all this filth."

"There's no need. Everything's just fine."

Fateema went over to the wooden table that had a gas stove on it. She put some tea to boil. Handing Kareema a cup, she poured some for herself.

"Any biscuits or bread around?"

"No, you want some? Should I go get them?"

"You really are the limit, Kareem. We're not going to live like this once I move in."

Fateema's equanimity unnerved Kareem.

"What do you mean, once you move in?"

"Of course, there'll be no hostel once I start on my post-graduation so later…"

"Later is later, we'll see about that. Now you better go: your rector will be screaming her head off."

"Not at all. I have informed her. Kareembhai, can't we buy our own little house once the two of us start earning? Away from this madness, a quiet little place where there are benches and a park." Niruben's house appeared before Fateeema's eyes.

"Get real, Fatee, we don't have that kind of money and even if we did… Never mind, you leave now." Kareem stood up.

Fateema's presence was unsettling. What was she talking about? Kareem was about to take off, to join Allah's army. Anwar had plans to send Kareem somewhere for training.

"Leave now, I need to study."

"Like I don't. Let's go." On her way out, Fateema asked, "Kareem, any news of Jamaal?"

"He's fine, working as a driver."

Many more questions bubbled up in Fateema's mind, but the answers she was receiving were horrifying. *Allah, I hope I am wrong.*

"*Pyaar kiya to darna kya,*" Komal hummed. She was convinced that she was in love with Mazhar. He had told her that his great-great-grandmother was British. He may also have had Greek ancestors because many soldiers who joined Alexander the Great from Greece had stayed back in Afghanistan. That explained why he was so fair and good-looking. Komal found this all very romantic. Mazhar was her hero now, and she had pretty much lost interest in her studies. Pappaji was never going to agree to a match between her and Mazhar. But what was love without rebellion? – and Komal hummed yet another song. Lying next to her, Fateema was oblivious. Komal didn't need her permission to go out with Mazhar: she had started using yoga classes as an excuse to go out during the day. Manuben was being given a cast-iron excuse. In any case, wasn't love also a kind of meditation? Fateema would never know this: all *she* did was read.

Komal had received a signal for love, and for nikaah. Mazhar would join his uncle's business in Muscat and eventually Komal would also join him. A desert can bloom with colour!

Preparations were underway. Rusted grills had been sawed and removed. Komal had cut them like through tree trunks. She would have waited until her examinations got over, but Mazhar had said, "You can appear for your exams after the nikaah." Komal loved the thought. In any case, Pappaji would have taken her home as soon as the exams were over.

It was about midnight. Soundlessly, Komal got up. Fateema was asleep. Komal didn't feel like leaving without saying goodbye to her dear friend. But what was the use? Fateema would not understand. Komal had finished all her preparations before Fateema returned from college. She had written a letter to Fateema, hidden the burkha under the pillow, put the mess-charges in an envelope with Manuben's name on it and left it on the dressing-table.

She now quietly placed the letter for Fateema next to the envelope. She filled a tiny bag with some clothes, put the burkha on and went to the window. The rusted and broken grill had been fully removed from the window frame. She jumped out of the window and landed with a thud.

The sound woke Fateema up. She immediately took a flashlight from her bedside table and switched it on. She saw the broken window and looked around. There was nobody in the room. Was that Komal then? Fateema rushed to the window. Komal stood there adjusting her burkha.

"Komal!"

Komal shushed her.

"What are you doing? Where are you going?"

Fateema did not need an answer. She saw a two-wheeler

in the hazy streetlight outside the hostel gates, and a figure lurking nearby. She was going to elope! Komal began to walk away briskly. Fateema also jumped over the window ledge. She ran after Komal and tried to grab her hand just as Komal neared the gate. The shadowy figure had hidden itself, she noticed. Meanwhile, Komal had climbed the iron gates and was trying to jump to the other side, but her burkha got entangled in the spikes.

"Komal, stop! What are you doing?"

"Fatee, let me go. My friend is waiting."

"Are you insane? Who is it?" Irritated, Komal tried to shrug off Fateema's hand while freeing her burkha. "It's none of your business."

"Yes, it is. Komal, come back, please."

Their voices reached a pitch and suddenly their faces were lit up. Manuben stood on the upper floor shining a torch on them. Everything was clear to her. She came down immediately.

Komal was still stuck on the gate. Fateema stood holding her hand.

"Girls, what is going on? You are running away with your lovers, right?" Manuben's voice was soft but vicious.

Fateema had never heard Manuben sound like this. What's more she seemed to include Fateema in the elopement plan. A stunned Fateema stood watching. Manuben pulled Komal off the gate, removed the burkha and shone the torch on her face.

"Komal? Is that you?" Turning towards Fateema she said, "Were you also eloping or helping her? You gave her your burkha to run off with one of your kind, didn't you?"

Manuben's voice cut through Fateema, ripping her to pieces. Fateema held the gate for support and Komal sat down hard on the floor.

A couple of other windows opened. Manuben told the girls to be quiet and ordered them inside.

Komal got up with great difficulty. She and Fateema went inside. They were about to go to their room, but Manuben hissed, "Not there. Upstairs."

Hesitantly, they climbed the stairs. Next to Manuben's quarters was a room where old files were stored. Manuben opened the door and pushed the girls inside. The room was dark.

"Stay here."

A pile of old newspapers lay in the corner. The two of them stood not knowing what to do. Manuben slammed the door shut and locked it.

Fateema was in a state of shock. She was like a homeless child whose house had been destroyed by the flood. Her reputation lay in smithereens. Manuben thought she was also responsible. And the one who was actually responsible for bringing Fateema to this state stood sobbing, and clinging to her.

"Fateema!"

"What 'Fateema'? I'm going to be blamed because of you…" Fateema broke down.

"What do we do now?"

"Keep quiet for now."

Komal's sobs had died down, as the minutes ticked by slowly into the night. Her head resting on Fateema's shoulder, she finally fell asleep.

Fateema sat, gazing at the fleeting shadows on the wall. Did Komal mean to run away? Who was the boy? Mazhar? And what would she have done after eloping? *She could at least have told me.*

Just as well Manuben caught her, otherwise this girl would have landed herself in a mess. Manuben thought it was my burkha! Arre, I don't even own a burkha. Who gave this to her? Mazhar? Was that really him? Kareem's friend? If Ba had known about this, all hell would have broken loose: "Scoundrels! Are you studying or destroying lives?"

Fateema dozed off.

The door to their room opened in the morning.

Fatigue, embarrassment and hunger had almost finished the two girls.

"Come with me."

Manuben's face was expressionless. The two girls followed her to the hostel office. Fateema's heart hammered against her chest. They stood rubbing their eyes and facing Manuben. Fateema glanced at the wall clock: half-past ten. All the girls must have left for college. Manuben had spared them the tamasha by confining them to the room.

"Is this what your parents sent you here for?" Manuben gave them a hard stare.

To Komal she said, "How old are you Komal? Nineteen? Twenty? That loser, whoever you were running away with, what would he have done to earn a living? Labour?"

"He loves me a lot." Komal raised her head.

"I see. Do you even know what love is?"

"…." Komal spouted some filmy cliché.

"Is that so? Let him go to your father and seek your hand."

"My father would kill him in a shot."

"So, he would not approve of this fellow?" Manuben put her hand gently on Komal's shoulder. "Love is about a new vision, not blindness. I know all about your so-called yoga classes now. I was keeping an eye on you, but I didn't expect…"

Then she turned to Fateema.

Sixteen

Fateema could barely raise her eyes to meet Manuben's. Of course, she could prove her innocence but she felt guilty that she had not tried hard enough to talk Komal out of it.

Manuben spoke. "Fateema, that I included you in my accusations against Komal was certainly unfair. After locking the two of you up, I went through your room and found the letter Komal had written." Waving the letter in front of Komal, she continued, "You did your roommate a huge favour by writing this letter. At least I now know that Fateema had no role in your elopement."

Fateema suddenly felt unburdened.

"In fact, Fateema tried to dissuade you." Manuben's voice faltered, tired. "Do you know, you silly girl, what you were trying to do? You would have ruined your life and the reputation I've spent decades building. How could I possibly have explained this to other parents and the trustees of the hostel?"

"I am sorry," Komal mumbled.

"Sorry? You think it's Fateema's job to look after you? She is here to make something out of her life. Thank her for having cared. Now leave." A resigned Manuben dismissed them.

The two girls tiptoed out of the room. Komal slumped on her bed. Anger, disappointment, sadness – what was she experiencing? Fateema neither knew nor cared. She lay down and closed her eyes.

A few days later, Komal's father came and took her away with him.

Meanwhile, Fateema was called to Manuben's office again one day. After thanking Fateema for classifying and sorting out the applications, Manuben said, "So Fateema, what are your plans now?"

"Jee, I would like do an M.A. after my B.A."

"Arre, that's lovely. I love it when girls carry on to higher studies. Anyway, do sit down. Why are you standing?" Manuben offered her a chair.

A hesitant Fateema sat down. Looking her in the eye, Manuben said, "Now listen, you are an adult and a mature person."

A bewildered Fateema wondered why Manuben was saying that. Had she done something?

Manuben laughed. "All I mean is sit straight and confidently. Look at me and speak up. You should understand the value of self-respect, you have studied in Navprabhat School after all. You have a right to be respected."

Fateema sat up straight.

Something flashed before her eyes. Sweets hidden in the odhni, the collision with Gaekwad Sir, the elocution prizes.... Yes, a lot had happened. She had made stepping-stones out of the debris of her life, and would continue to do so.

"In all this I have not even asked you what subjects you are studying for your B.A."

"History and Anthropology."

"Such interesting things you youngsters study, you are indeed fortunate. Our parents allowed us to do Matriculation and Hindi examinations, that was it. We considered ourselves lucky, although even this much turned out to be helpful."

The peon brought some tea. Fateema understood what Manuben meant by behaving like an equal, and drinking tea with her across the table. She excused herself after tea.

"Manuben, thank you."

"Listen, Ben, let me tell you finally why I called you here. I put in a word with Patel Saaheb for you. You'll be able to stay in the hostel until you finish your Masters. He confirmed it today."

Fateema wanted to dance for joy. She ended up saying 'thanks,' but walked over to Manuben and bowed her head with a namaste. "I had tea with you, but it's only appropriate to do a namaskar now."

"Off you go, and stop worrying," Manuben laughed. She mumbled to herself, "I should be saying thank *you*."

As Fateema left the office, she was convinced that there was a guardian angel looking out for her. Four years of confirmed accomodation! She could concentrate on her studies now. A well-paid job and a house, that's it. She could bring Ba to town then. *She'll be able to sit on the swing in my balcony…*

Fateema knew this fantasy was not the only thing pushing her towards education. She was deeply interested in the subjects she was studying, although she didn't know when the seeds of History had been sown in her. Then there were good, interested teachers. Dilip Shah had the class rolling with laughter on the very first day.

"My name is Dilip Shah – a perfectly ordinary, common-as-muck name. All you have to do is to shout 'Dilipbhai' in any of the housing societies of Bombay, and you'll have ten people craning their necks to answer. It's that common. But I will teach you some of the most difficult names, names such as Nebuchadnezzar, his son Belshazzar, Hittites and Senacharib. You want more? Well, you have over two years to memorize all this. For now, take it easy."

Another professor asked everybody's date of birth. Many students were born in June or July.

"I just knew it. People with particular zodiac signs are the only ones to end up in, I mean with, History."

The instructors tried hard to make History interesting, although Fateema was often asked, "Arre ben, what kind of ancient subject is this? Something contemporary gets a quicker job."

Fateema knew that of course. But she would reply flippantly, "Look at Laila with Majnu's eyes."

The college was on the outskirts of the city. The library building was the last one on campus.

Getting a BA was not that difficult: you could get by with a few weeks of preparation just before the exams. Many students did their Bachelor's degree and also worked part-time. Fateema gave tuitions in the evenings. The rest of the time she spent in the library, reading books.

The librarian, Rachel David, liked passing on new books to Fateema.

"Fateemaben."

"Call me Fateema, please."

"All right, Fateema, I have something for you if you have the time." She handed her a book – *The Bible as History*.

Fateema dipped into it, and found it absorbing. She sat by the window and read. A civilization going back by a thousand years came into her view. The Bible was not only religious, but also historical. Archaeologists had dug up Biblical sites and found evidence of its time and people. Rachel stood behind Fateema.

"It's great, isn't it?" she said.

"Rachel, I am really enjoying it."

"I am Jewish, and you a Muslim. The region this book talks about witnessed other religions even before yours and mine. We tend to claim antiquity for our religion, but that's not true. Other people lived there who also had their gods. Read it, Fateema, but also make notes, maybe they'll come in handy some day."

Neither Fateema nor Rachel knew how prescient her comments were. Perhaps Allah had made her say those words. Fateema went back to reading the book, making notes, and studying maps.

The Bible is the story of Christ. Where was he born? There you go. This is Egypt, this the Mediterranean Sea, this is what is now Israel, and this is Jerusalem. It was from this sacred point that Angel Gabriel took the Prophet, and brought him back. Who were these people? Farmers? They travelled by boat and on camels. This land between Egypt and Asia was called Canaan. It was just a narrow strip of land, but one that witnessed historic upheavals. Here many wars were waged in the name of religion.

The inhabitants of this region were literate. They developed a script. People made letters out of wet earth and baked them in kilns. Engraved monuments tell stories of spies and soldiers, appeals for a hike in salaries, eulogies for the powerful. All in all, there seemed to have been a modern and layered administration.

Fateema continued to read – of desert lands and nomadic tribes, their encroachment upon settled civilizations. She saw patterns that cut across the stories of many civilizations. Amid fears of robbery and pillage, people created poetry and sculpture too.

On the way back to the hostel, while Fateema was thinking about the book, she felt her universe had expanded, and that she herself had changed.

"What planet are you on, Fateema?" Manuben asked.

"Sorry? Oh, I've been busy with the final exams."

"Enough now. Stop reading all day. It will drive you insane. Come with me, let's go to the Sunday market."

"Really, Manuben!"

"Look at other girls in this hostel, they can't see anything beyond films and shopping, whereas you don't go anywhere at all. Where's your brother these days by the way?"

"Somewhere in North India. He has a good job though. His friend keeps calling me with updates."

On Sunday morning, Fateema left with Manuben for Gujari Bazaar, the Sunday market. An excited Manuben said, "You get all kinds of things here. Once, a friend of mine came across an idol of the Buddha."

The Sunday market was on the banks of the river. Its wares ranged from old household things, second-hand electronic items, old clothes and old books to antiques, photoframes, beaded necklaces and lamps.

As many objects as people – haggling, talking, rubbing shoulders with each other and creating both the music and the cacophony of life. The sun's rays fell sharply on Fateema's body, but it was December, and the warmth felt good. She and Manuben watched in fascination. They walked and looked about until they reached the sliver-like river. It had suddenly become luminous and as Fateema looked up, it caught the sun and the water below shimmered like a river of light.

Fateema's heart lurched on seeing such beauty. She didn't know Arabic well, but she had begun to read it in English translation. Unbidden, these lines came to her mind:

And thus it is with most people if thou ask them, 'What is it that has created the heavens and the earth and made the Sun and Moon subservient to his laws they will surely answer, "Allah!"

And thus it is if thou ask them who is it that sendeth down water from the skies, giving life thereby to the earth after it had been lifeless? They will surely answer, "Allah."

"Are you lost again? Chalo, Fateema, you'll get sunstroke."

"Alright, but there are some stalls on that side…" The two of them walked off in the other direction, away from the sun. A little ahead, they saw a man who had spread out a mat with pictures, idols, and pooja paraphernalia arranged on it. Manuben headed towards him, but came to a sudden stop.

"I'm sorry," she said to Fateema.

"What for?"

"I was going to ask you to take a look at these idols and pictures, but then I remembered you people don't believe in this, right?"

"True. The Prophet prohibits idol worship," Fateema replied.

"So you wait here in the shade. I'll take a quick look and come back."

Fateema laughed.

"I'll come with you. I may not believe in it, but surely I can appreciate idols as works of art, right? And who knows, you may get lost in this crowd."

At the stall, Manuben laid her hands upon a slight torn-at-the-edge but otherwise intact and beautiful picchwai.

"Arre, how lovely this is." Manuben sat down to look at other things as well. Clearly a family moving to a new house had discarded invaluable things as trash. Manuben picked up five or six objects, haggled and finally paid up. They returned to the hostel, Manuben happy about the bargains she had struck and Fateema happy about a new world she had got to see.

The sun had tired Fateema out. But she had gone beyond the walled library to an unknown invisible world. Suddenly it occurred to her that her Baapu did the same business! He went around people's homes collecting scrap. He sold his wares exactly like this. As Fateema lay down on her hostel bed, she couldn't help thinking of her father's life, his swollen feet and his bicycle. How much he had struggled to the end so that his children could live a better life. He had helped them jump the fence of poverty and illiteracy.

✳

Fateema took a deep breath and washed her face with cold water. She came out of the room. She felt very sad. She heard the girls laughing and clapping in the TV room and went and joined them. They were busy watching a comedy show. They moved and made room for her to sit.

Fateema also found the programme amusing. The comedy was followed by filmy dances, star-studded shows and glittering women. Suddenly the dances stopped.

Breaking News.

A bomb had exploded in Ujjain, outside a Shiv temple where a festival was held every year. Many devotees were wounded, some had died. The news showed footage of violence and misery for the next few minutes. No harm had come to the temple or the Shivling in it.

The girls who had been laughing uproariously minutes ago were now in a state of shock. Anger gathered itself in the group.

"How cruel these people are, murderers!"

"Arre, their religion is like that…"

"Killing innocent people!"

"Shh…" The girls suddenly registered Fateema's presence. The TV was switched off, and everyone dispersed wordlessly.

Fateema went back to her room. If only she could show those women how much of a burden she carried. She opened her diary and began writing:

"The jihad as mentioned by the Prophet is a war against injustice and oppression. Islam means peace and surrender. Islam does not recommend killing innocent people. The Prophet released hundreds of slaves from bondage and sent them back to their native land."

There was a lot more she could write. She would one day. Not for others, but to her own people she would explain the meaning of 'Islam'.

Seventeen

How did the wheel of time turn so fast? She had barely entered college, and she was already a BA! She wrote her last exam and came out. There were droves of students outside the examination centre engaged in intense discussions about which film to watch, or which restaurant to go to.

Fateema stood under a tree waiting to be picked up by Kareem. The plan was to have dinner with him at his kholi.

"You've been back for a fortnight, and I didn't even know!" Fateema was angry.

"Because of your exams." With this, Kareem had hung up.

Fateema was to spend that evening with Kareem and leave to visit Ba the following day. She had a very short break. She had to come back to start tuitions for two children that Rachel had helped her find. Fateema was to give lessons in English. The extra money she earned during the vacations was always welcome: she had two more years of hostel accommodation to pay for.

Kareem walked towards her. Fateema covered her head with a dupatta. There was no point in fighting, the two siblings were meeting each other after a year or so. Kareem was wearing a white pathani, a skullcap and pathani sandals, and he sported a beard. Fateema rode pillion on his two-wheeler.

Kareem dropped her at his house and disappeared. Fateema cleaned the room up. Ants scurried about in the little kitchen. The ceiling was full of cobwebs. Fateema took a broom and cleared everything up. Then she headed to the grocery store round the corner. As she walked, she heard someone call her.

"Kareembhai's sister?"

Fateema turned around and noticed a woman at a window in one of the houses.

"Yes?"

The window closed and a door opened. "Come inside, na?"

Fateema hesitated, but she did go inside the house. She saw a depressing, poorly lit room. No sign of children – perhaps they had gone to a madrasa. There were three or four women in the centre of the room, their hands busy embroidering. Fateema was made to sit on a plastic chair.

"I have seen you a couple of times, so I called you over." The woman smiled a little. "My name is Shakila. And yours?"

"Fateema."

"This is my daughter, Saira." Saira, who also held embroidery needles and cloth, looked down. A gentle smile played upon her lips. She reminded Fateema of her own sister.

"I had a sister who went away to be with Allah. Her name was also Saira." Fateema's voice was gentle.

Saira looked up with a confident smile on her face. She was fair-skinned and radiant, Fateema thought. Shakila signalled something to one of the women who brought a cold drink. Fateema didn't know why she had been invited in. She had not been a regular visitor to Kareem's house. In the meantime, Shakila fired off questions about Kareem's education and employment. Fateema now understood the motive behind the invitation. She noticed that Saira kept her eyes lowered throughout, listening to every word intently.

Fateema did not have adequate answers for all of Shakeela's questions. Job? I don't know. Salary? I don't know.

"Would you please find out, Fateemaben?" Shakila requested.

As she got up to leave, Fateema asked, "What does Saira study?"

Shakila proudly raised her head. "Arre, she can read the Koran in Arabic."

Fateema wished them Khuda Hafiz and left.

Of course every Muslim must know how to read the Koran in Arabic. But something nagged at her. Was this much education enough? How would she explain to someone like Shakila that times had changed, and would continue to do so? *Without an education, English and technology, how was our quam to do better? How much would these women earn with their embroidery? Will my poor Muslim sisters spend their lives like this?* These thoughts stayed with Fateema as she turned back to go to Kareem's kholi after picking up a disinfectant from a grocery store. She sprayed the house, shut it and sat outside on the otla, surrounded for a while by bickering children. She went back inside and carried on cleaning. For a moment she felt mad at Kareem, but also wondered how he could have kept the house clean in such a filthy neighbourhood. It had also been lying unused for over a year.

Kareem arrived late in the evening with Anwar. They had brought food as well. Fateema laid out the plates and the three of them sat down to eat.

"Any news of Mazhar?" Anwar asked during dinner.

"No, I think he has gone to Hyderabad. He's not likely to even call now," Kareem replied.

"He's unnecessarily scared. I checked, nobody has made a complaint against him."

They suddenly fell quiet, aware of Fateema's presence.

"What's that smell?" Kareem asked.

"I sprayed the house. Kareembhai, if your education is over, get somebody to look after you. At least the house will remain clean and occupied." Fateema laughed. "You will be staying here, I presume?"

"Not sure. Let's see, some education is yet to finish." Anwar replied on behalf of Kareem. He seemed to know more.

Fateema was suddenly reminded of Shakila.

"Kareembhai, you are under observation, I don't think you know that."

Kareem jumped out of his skin.

"Wh—at? Me? How do you know?"

Anwar and Kareem stared at Fateema intently.

Fateema laughed. "I was taken to the surveillance party's house and offered a soft drink today. There were detailed inquiries about you. Your movements seem to be well known in the neighbourhood!"

Kareem's face looked pinched with worry.

"Who was it? What did you tell them?"

"Me? Oh, I told them everything that I knew." Fateema was having fun.

"What do you mean? What do you know? Fateema, what did you say, tell me!" Kareem's questions were relentless. He dug his fingers into her arm.

"Kareem, gently please. Fateemaji, tell us properly. Who are you talking about? What did they ask you?"

Fateema wriggled out of Kareem's grip, surprised at how seriously they were treating her light-heartedness.

"What is all this, Kareem? You're acting like the cops are after you. Why are you so anxious?"

"Cops?" Kareem's voice was fearful.

"Yes bhai, this is the mohalla police. A mother who wants to get her daughter married is as bad as a cop. She's got her eye on you." Fateema smiled indulgently.

The two men were not amused. "Cut the jokes," Kareem said, curtly.

Fateema told them about Shakila and her daughter. She added, "Saira is good, Kareem. She will go along with your thinking."

Anwar and Kareem looked more relaxed now.

After dinner the two men sat outside on plastic chairs. Fateema was inside washing the dishes. Her hands froze as their words fell upon her ears.

"The girl was trying to run away, but her plans were ruined because another girl saw her eloping."

Who were they talking about? Komal? How do these men know?

"You should have gone that day, Kareem."

"No, Anwarbhai, I am glad I didn't. If the cops had got involved, there would have been other complications."

"True. We still have a long way to go."

"We could have told Fateema…"

"No, Kareem, we need Fateema for a lot of things. She shouldn't be involved in this." Anwar's voice sounded strange to Fateema.

"That's fine."

"I tell you what, Kareem, catch hold of schools. Ammiji is right about this. For younger ones films, money, jewellery make it easier. Before they can think, they can be made to do a nikaah. That's how we embolden our faith."

What was Anwar talking about? Were they really talking of entrapping girls? And who the hell was this Ammiji?

The following day, Fateema left to visit Ba. The village had changed since her last visit. The lane leading to her house was dotted with signs like 'Lucky Pavbhaji House' and 'Jolly Tea House.' The houses also looked different. From a distance, the school building looked the same. Would Gaekwad Sir and Jani Sir be around? She must find out.

She stood at the threshold. Thanks to Kareem's efforts, the house looked well maintained. She knocked at the door. Then, realizing that Ba's hearing may have failed, she knocked louder, feeling somewhat apprehensive. The door opened. Ba stood there. She looked the same, just a little older, a little more helpless and yet still very strong. She exuded the confidence of a lone and self-reliant person.

"Alee, you think I have gone deaf, knocking madly at the door?" Ba said to her.

Fateema laughed and hugged her mother. Holding Fateema's hand, Ba walked into the house. "These wretched knees are letting me down, so it takes me time to get up."

Fateema put her suitcase in a corner. She made Ba sit on a chair and gave her some water. It was Fateema who, after seeing the paniyaru in Chandan's house, had insisted on having one in her own. She and Ba-Baapu had built one together. It was chipped at the edges now, but intact. The mud and brass pots were Ba's property.

Fateema would take both with them once she had a house of her own. There'd be a paniyaru in her house as well.

After lunch, the mother and daughter lay down next to each other on a string cot. Running her fingers through Fateema's hair, Ba said, "Your hair looks less wild now." And then it dawned upon her, "Arre, did you cut it? So short?"

"Ba, should I be spending time studying or taming my wild hair everyday?"

"Of course, of course."

Fateema told her all about the hostel, and the trip to Gujari Bazaar with Manuben.

"Nice. Take me along some day, if my wretched knees will let me!"

"They will let you, Ba, they will. If they don't, I'll take you in a wheelchair."

The thought of a chair moving along on wheels made Ba giggle.

They talked about the village and its people. Ba did not ask her even once when she would finish studying, or what Kareem was doing.

And then, suddenly she said, "That Jamaaliyo is in Mumbai, you know!"

"Really? Did he call?" Fateema asked.

"No phone-vone here, silly girl. He sent me a message through someone that he was in Mumbai and working in phillim."

Jamaal in films? I thought he was a driver.

Then Ba wanted to tell her something else, but only if Fateema promised not to laugh.

"Some months ago, your schoolwallahs came to pick me up. Oh bhai, it was such a big programme! They put a shawl around me and Narbadaben. And they gave me this chakardu." Ba pointed to the ledge.

Fateema stood up and went up to the ledge. She saw a memento given to Ba on behalf of the village. Ba had been felicitated for helping the village people through difficult times. When Jani Sir's daughter had cancer, it was Ba who had nursed the ailing girl in her final days. Jani Sir's wife had arthritis so she was of no help. But Ba had also made opium tablets for Jani Sir's wife and given her medicine at regular intervals. She was free, she told Jani Sir. "You go and teach children," she said to him. "Poor kids need to study."

Fateema's eyes were misty. She was proud to be this mother's daughter.

Four or five days went by. She went to the school and met the teachers. Gaekwad Sir ordered tea for her. Fateema was reminded of Manuben's advice. She sat across from Gaekwad Sir and talked about college and hostel. How could she forget the reference letter he had provided her, which is what got her admission into the hostel? Jani Sir was on leave: he had taken his wife for ayurvedic treatment. Fateema relived some old memories with other teachers as well – Smitaben, Geetaben and others. Geetaben asked her, "Do you only study or have you also found a 'friend?'"

Why did Fateema think of Anwar?

She chatted with the teachers about Kareem as well. It was particularly heartwarming to see the school though. An entire room had been dedicated to computer training, there was an audio-visual room and there were plans for a swimming pool and gymnasium.

Fateema had come for her visit to the village joyfully and she was leaving happily. *Bas, two more years, inshallah.*

The bus returned from the village. Ba had insisted on seeing her off at the bus stand once again. When the bus hit the highway, words like 'tofaan' 'hullad' and 'chhurabaaji' could be heard. As the bus drove on, torched buses, shops and broken glass began to come into view. The passengers sat, curled up in fear. Communal violence had broken out in the city.

The passengers looked at each other fearfully. Who was a Hindu in this bus? Who was a Muslim? Which side will attack the bus? People began making noises about each other's religion. It looked like an inter-religious riot would have broken out in the bus, but Fateema stood up and addressed everyone, "Please, for the terrible acts of a handful of people, let's not malign an entire community. Remember, all of us have to reach the same stop." There was some commotion, then everyone fell silent.

Suddenly, the tyres screeched, the driver braked suddenly and the bus came to a halt. The passengers craned their necks out of the windows to see what was happening. A group of 'troublemakers' boarded the bus wielding torches, swords and hockey sticks. The passengers sat down. Women covered their faces with saris and dupattas. Men began covering their wives and daughters. A young man's eyes scanned the bus, finding most people to be simple village folk. His eyes came to rest on Fateema.

"Which religion? What's your name?"

A surge of terror coursed through Fateema's body. She looked around. She saw an old woman in a black sari.

"My name is Falobai," Fateema answered. With her head lowered, she spoke in rural Gujarati, "We are all together."

"She is with me," the woman confirmed.

"Falobai? Hindu or Muslim?" the young man asked.

"What do you think? Look at yourself and tell us what you look like," Fateema said, once again in dialect.

"Eh bai, stop this bakbak, and answer."

"What do I tell you? You want to hear the story of Sati Narbada, or of Parsotam mother? We are all from the same village. What do you want to do? Kill us all?"

The young men standing near the bus were about to douse the bus with petrol: nothing was going to make them change their minds. Just then a police siren began to wail. The young man jumped off the bus and the bunch of ruffians standing below beat a hasty retreat.

"Nobody light up beedis or cigarettes in the bus," the driver warned and accelerated away.

The passengers sat in stunned silence. Someone said, "This Faloben is something!"

At night, Manuben laughed when she heard Fateema's story. "Falo, Fateema Lokhandwala, wow!"

"But Manuben, if that woman had not backed me up and said that I was with her, what would have happened to me? Honestly, that was an angel in a black sari."

"Indeed, ben. We forget that we are together," Manuben said, simply.

That night, Fateema prayed for everyone.

Eighteen

"Ammiji wants to see you."

Fateema was through with lectures. She came out of the college building and saw Kareem standing outside.

"Let's go."

"But who is Ammiji?" Fateema asked. Why would a stranger want to meet her? "Does she need me for some drafting, for writing something?"

"Stop asking questions. Just tell Manuben that you will be late."

"That's not needed anymore."

Ammiji – a tall woman with rimless spectacles, hennaed hair, a green sari with a zari border, glittering gold bangles and a gold chain. She was regal, just like the begum of a small Muslim kingdom in Uttar Pradesh. She sat on a sofa with Anwar next to her.

Kareem nudged Fateema to do the aadab. Ammiji responded to Fateema's greeting with an "Alekum Salaam." Fateema felt the weight of Ammiji's eyes upon her, as she was examined head to toe. A quiet exchange of looks followed between Ammiji and her son.

Ammiji had checked into a company guesthouse. The guesthouse chef had laid out many spicy dishes before them. Fateema felt assaulted by the masala.

"Arre, why aren't you eating anything? *Bahaut accha khana bana hai*," Anwar said.

"Thank you. I am fine."

"Is Ammiji's presence making you self-conscious?" Anwar's tone held a new familiarity. *What is going on here?* Fateema asked herself. The conversation veered towards tastes in food, Ammiji's preferences, and questions of what Fateema liked and so on. Ammiji was new to the city so Fateema was entrusted with the responsibility of taking her shopping. Fateema found herself swept along by a new and unknown current.

So far she had been given no choice in the matter. The question did not arise. Carrying food out of Chandan's house in the torn folds of a dupatta was a vivid memory, but this plenitude was new – to be shown dozens of new clothes in shops and say, "I don't like anything" and leave. Why not though? Fateema was Anwar's choice. It was evident that Kareem was happy about this.

"Fateema, you stay with Ammiji for a few days," Kareem said to her that night. It was a command.

After dinner, Ammiji, Fateema, Kareem and Anwar sat on the verandah. Ammiji prepared a paan for each of them.

"Now listen, I have spoken to Manuben and taken special permission," Kareem informed her. Fateema had no reason protest.

"Permission? What for?" Ammiji asked.

"It's a hostel Ammiji, how would they let a girl go out without making sure, right?" Anwar explained. Ammiji looked happy with the explanation.

"Of course. Girls shouldn't have too much liberty." Ammiji spoke in a mixture of Hindi and Gujarati. Did she also visit Gujarat often, like Anwar? Now was not the time to ask questions. She was fortunate to have had the opportunity of a meal with such an aristocratic family.

"Did Manuben agree?"

"Of course. Would she dare say no to me?" Kareem replied.

"I see…" She felt something jab at her. "But my college?"

"Forget it. This is more important. Anyway, it's only a matter of four or five days, at least for now."

The following morning was beautiful. Breakfast was served under a canopy. Ammiji and Anwar appeared to be late risers. (If Ba was around, she would have said, "they don't have to go looking for dung cakes in the morning!") Fateema began reading the newspaper.

After breakfast, Fateema and Ammiji left in a long white car to go shopping. An exotic and ornate world of clothes and jewellery unfolded before them. A row of salesmen stood waiting to serve Fateema and Ammiji.

Piles of saris were brought out, black, white and red, and resplendent with gold embroidery. Ammiji made her selection and ordered them to be polished. Anwar was to make the payment later. "Fateema, you choose some now."

A flustered Fateema replied, "Jee… I don't know, how will I ever wear these clothes? I only need a simple salwar kameez for college, and maybe a sari or two…"

Ammiji looked astonished.

"How does college come into the picture?"

Fateema did not reply. What could she say? These were two different worlds. Happiness swung in this world like the little domes of gold earrings, and power lay in the clinking of golden bangles.

One day, another day, Kareem had hinted at her nikaah with Anwar.

"Kareem, at least tell me their full names. I don't even know that!"

Kareem laughed. "You'd faint if I told you their last name. They are way up in class."

So was she to give up her studies? Rachel and the library continued to wait for her. Over the next few days she noticed that the guesthouse received many visitors who sat on the garden chairs and discussed things with the rest.

Fateema wanted to join in. They looked like educated people. It would be good to listen to what they had to say.

Ammiji's forehead twisted in a frown. "What nonsense, Fateema. How can a Muslim woman be sitting next to unknown men?"

Fateema was staggered. Ammiji calmed down somewhat. "Listen beti, you are educated. But try to understand the quam you belong to: learn its do's and don'ts."

"Sorry."

Fateema looked longingly at the balcony adjacent to her room. It overlooked the garden. She would have liked to sit there and read. She didn't have to be told that a book in her hand would irritate both Anwar and Ammiji. Kareem had warned her.

Fateema would riffle through Ammiji's fashion magazines. Words like 'jihad,' 'training camp,' 'oil money' and 'Palestine' would fall on her ears. What are these people talking about? One day, a visitor said as he was about to leave, "Anwar, enough now. It's time to begin work. There are constant inquiries from above about whether Kareem is ready."

"I know. We will start now, we just need to pick up four or five boys."

"All right. Just remember that a lot of money is being spent, something needs to happen now." So saying, the visitor left.

What work? Pick up four or five boys, meaning what?

Fateema was too stunned to think. Did she hear what she thought she'd heard? No, that was not possible. They must have been talking about a Muslim jamaat and the 'work' must be about helping people in the quam, Fateema told herself.

After five or six days, Fateema started to become restless. Arre, she hadn't even been allowed to step out of her room yesterday. She must go to college now.

Fateema got ready early the next morning. Ammiji had not woken up. A surprised servant gave her tea and toast. After breakfast, she simply left for college. College was like homecoming. Fateema felt free and happy.

In the college building, the peon asked her to go to the staff room. Dr Dilip Shah was waiting for her.

"Hello Fateemaben, you've been missing. All well, I hope?"

"Sir, I…" Before Fateema could finish, he cut in, "Now listen, I need your help for a paper on the common roots of Islam, Judaism and Christianity. I would like to present this in a national seminar for history teachers. People know very little about this subject, and Islam in particular is considered only a jihadi religion. I don't mean to hurt your sentiments, but the fact of the matter is that you must prepare at least a rough outline on this in the next few days."

"Few days?"

"All right, all right. Take a week then. Max." Fateema loved such assignments. It wasn't a burden at all. In fact, she and Rachel had meant to write something like this together. Never mind if Dr Shah got all the credit. It's only natural that teachers take advantage of bright students.

An hour later and Fateema was in the library with a pile of books in front of her. Yes, she would expose all the misconceptions about Islam.

A fifteen-page article? Arre, how was she to manage to cram more than two thousand years of history into fifteen pages? It began with Abraham; he and his wife left Mesopotamia and settled down in Canaan-Israel. All three religions – Judaism, Christianity and Islam – consider Abraham their patriarch. Abraham and his wife Sara had a late child. God asked Abraham to slay his child. Abraham raised the knife to obey God's command. But that was only to test his faith in God. Abraham was the father of Judaism.

Many centuries later, Judaism fell into the hands of oppressive religious leaders. It needed purification. Jesus was sent to do this. For about three hundred years after his crucifixion, Christianity, the religion established through Jesus's sacrifice, spread across the world. Jesus was a Jew, but his followers were Christians. Until about 7th century of the Common Era, Judaism and Christianity continued to be the only two monotheistic religions.

"There's somebody to see you." Rachel brought Fateema back to the present.

Fateema came out of the library, expecting Kareem. He stood there, with a face and voice equally harsh: "Come."

It was a command – and Fateema did not like it one bit. But this was not the place for argument. She said to him softly, "My Professor has given me an assignment. I need to get that ready."

"Have you gone berserk? You are refusing to come?"

"What do you mean? I have my studies."

"Stop this nonsense. Ammiji is waiting for you. You left without a by-your-leave."

"What should I have told her? She's a guest here, I've got my lectures to attend. How long can I keep missing them?"

Kareem tightened his grip on her arm. "You'll come with me. I will talk to you later."

They flagged a rickshaw and headed towards the guesthouse. Kareem took a deep breath.

"Fateema, you don't seem to understand."

"So make me."

"Ammiji and Anwar are not ordinary people."

"They are rich, that's obvious."

"Your tongue is wagging these days. They are leaders of the Islamic Union, soldiers of Islam. They want to spread the message of the Prophet everywhere, *saari duniya*."

"That's not a bad idea."

"Glad you think so. We are also soldiers." Fateema did not comment. She knew for certain that Kareem was speaking in a borrowed tongue.

Suddenly, something occurred to her. Was that what he had gone to North India for? Was Kareem studying there, or...

The words 'terrorist camp' flashed into her mind, and were pushed away just as quickly.

Anwar and Ammiji were waiting for her. The evening cast shadows upon the lawns of the guesthouse. Dressed in a green salwar, hijaab and gold jewellery, Ammi waited. The servant brought tea for Fateema.

Ammiji said to her, "Fateema, let's go. Freshen up quickly."

"Go where?"

"Kareem has made the arrangements. There's a lecture by Moulviji from Rahimnagar. Anwar will also be speaking."

"You will also speak." Kareem added.

"*Me?* What about?"

"You know very well what. Just get ready now." Kareem left to get ready.

"I have ordered a burkha for you. If you don't like burkhas, at least wear a hijaab. Go now. You too, Anwar."

Ammiji left to go to her room. Fateema was tempted to make an excuse and not join them. But she was also curious to know what such meetings were about.

When Kareem came out of his room he had changed his clothes and combed his beard.

"Ammiji is so modern. She has given permission for you to speak to other men at the majlis. Now women also need to become martyrs."

Anwar came and stood beside them. He watched Fateema closely.

Kareem continued, "Next month you and Anwar have a nikaah. So you shouldn't mind his presence."

Fateema was at her wits' end. All this was happening too fast. *Anwar, my husband? Arre, shouldn't Ba be told? Or at least asked? And what about me for heaven's sake?*

Ammiji appeared. "Chalo, Moulviji is waiting."

Fateema fled to get the hijab.

She saw several children, no more eight or ten years old. Each one wore a skull cap and white pathani suit. There were little girls as well, covered in black from head to toe.

Moulvi held forth on the history of Islam. Fateema liked that: it was exactly what she had been working on through the day. The Koran was revealed to the Prophet, moulvi explained. His eyes met Ammiji's, probably confirming whether Ammiji and Anwar liked his speech. Moulviji's voice went up by several decibels... *Jihad.*

Nineteen

Moulviji's eyes sparked, and he clenched his fists. "Jihad means battle – a battle against those who do not believe in Allah. Now listen."

With this, the moulvi began to narrate the Prophet's flight from Mecca to Medina and how the Prophet's wife, brother, friend and a slave were to become the first four Muslims, and how the Kuresh of Mecca thirsted for the Prophet's blood and mounted a war upon him. His summary was eloquent:

"Children, jihad continues even today. We are not afraid of bloodshed. We filled up the unholy lanes of Kolkata with dead bodies. We played a carnival of blood in Lahore. Arre, even my little child will learn how to make bombs, and blow up buildings. Our religion teaches us to attain martyrdom. Allah Ho Akbar!

"Children, jihad continues even today. Palestine and Kashmir, Jerusalem and Afghanistan... Jihad..."

Moulviji's words shot through the room like an electric current. If a single lecture could shake an educated woman like Fateema, is it surprising then that ordinary religious mobs are inspired to do battle? Ammiji and Anwar were spellbound. Kareem had occupied a chair outside the room. Fateema understood that he was keeping an eye out for unwanted visitors.

Ammiji signalled Anwar, who obediently stood up. He

went up to the microphone, greeted everybody with an aadab and said, "*Bache, tum abhi kacche ho*." Children laughed at his joke. "Nevertheless, after listening to Moulviji, even I feel I want to go on a jihad. Now, I invite Fateemaji to say something to you. She is an educated person, so listen to her carefully."

He beckoned Fateema over to take the microphone. She felt the ground beneath her feet shake: this eloquent woman, who gave speeches in school and received prizes, was at a loss for words.

A 'jihad' played itself out inside her now: an internal battle – a battle with meanness.

Of course, she could speak the way Anwar wanted her to, and that would bring an end to all her financial burdens, her anxiety to study and work. It would give her a lifetime of rest. Dressed in glittering jewellery, she would live the life of a rich wife of a rich man. Fateema, a life of luxury was only a few words away.

She adjusted her hijaab and took the microphone. She greeted everybody with "Salaam Alekum" and heard herself saying, *Fateema, you must only say what you want to say*. Of course.

"Children, I can't add much more to what Moulviji has already told you about Islam. But I will talk to you about jihad. As Anwarji mentioned, you are young and innocent. It's a good thing though that you are getting to learn the real essence of our religion so early on. Children, the Koran says, 'Oh Muhammad, you do a jihad with Koran.' This does not mean that the Koran is a sword or a gun. What it means is that, holding the sacred Koran in your hand and the lessons of peace and honesty in mind, you wage a war against evil.

"Children, should you need to fight to preserve your self-respect and your body, the Koran asks you to announce that to even your enemies. To kill innocents and cause harm to life and property is prohibited by the Koran."

Fateema paused, or was she made to? Taking the microphone away from her, Anwar said, "Thank you. These kids are much too young for such weighty arguments. They don't need to understand this."

On the way back to the guesthouse, Fateema was quiet. She knew that she was bidding goodbye to a life of luxury. As the car entered the guesthouse compound, Ammiji broke the silence: "Wrong, all wrong."

Not a sound was heard in the guesthouse. Fateema had a special air-conditioned room with beautiful rugs. But sleep eluded her.

She gently opened the door and came out of her room to sit on the verandah. Kareem's room lit up and she saw him coming out. In the hazy light of the evening, Kareem in his chequered lungi seemed like a stranger. He came and sat before Fateema, eyes seething with rage. Fateema took a deep breath and said, "I need to talk to you."

Kareem's eyes flickered towards Anwar's room. It was silent and dark.

Fateema's voice betrayed disappointment: "Kareem, what is all this? What on earth are you up to? How can you actually support such terrorism?"

Kareem gritted his teeth and hissed, "Come to my room."

She followed him, feeling that she should have asked him this question ages ago. Kareem signalled her to sit on the bed while he stood next to the window.

"Okay, now tell me, what is all this?" she started. "Have you given up your education? What about your degree?"

"I will get my degree. And I have not given up studying. Anwar has promised to help me get ahead."

"But who is this Anwar? Why have you made him such a close friend?"

"We are not friends. We are mujjahids." Kareem came over to where Fateema was and she made room for him to sit.

"Fateema, Anwar visited our college. He came looking for a science teacher to teach at a school in Lucknow. We got to know each other. He said he needed a science teacher because the subsequent battle is not going to be on a battleground, but in a laboratory. He wants me to go to England to learn nuclear science."

Fateema was petrified.

"You mean, what? What are you guys planning to do?"

"Fateema, our battle is on. We won Byzantium, defeated Darius of Persia, came through the Khyber Pass and established the Mughal rule. Once again…" Kareem's words were like balls of fire. Fateema stopped him.

"Enough, Kareem."

It was clear that Kareem had been brainwashed.

"You are also with us, don't you understand? Stop spewing such shit on the microphone now. Anwar told me the moment he met me that we need some educated women with us. You must support him."

Fateema sighed. She didn't say anything for a while, then softly, "Kareem, not only you, but thousands of scientists like you are needed for our country as well as rest of the world. Half of this country's population is Muslim and poor. They need soldiers like you."

Kareem stood up. "Stop pontificating. What are you trying to tell me, hanh?"

Fateema looked at Kareem. They were siblings living in a tiny village years ago. The house roof had innumerable holes in it. Moonlight fell through the cracks onto the floor.

The siblings chased moonbeams, the winner shouting, "My moon, my moon!" Kareem appeared to have held the moon in his fist today. He was not Kareem anymore. However she continued.

"Pontificating is better than stabbing, Kareem. Just as you are a science student, I am a student of history. History tells us that people have lived centuries before Judaism, Christianity and Islam appeared. They had also toiled and lived. So doesn't this country belong to them as well?"

Kareem twisted her arm. "Shut up, will you? No more college, you are now marrying Anwar. You will say what he lets you say."

Fateema headed back to her room. The past flickered before her eyes when Rajab Ali had decided upon her nikaah. She had furtively made a call to her teachers. She was rescued by her teachers that day and they had convinced her Baapu. But whom could she call today?

Fateema started putting her books and films in a plastic bag. She put away the clothes Ammiji had bought for her.

The following day there was another meeting near Navapur, a youth convention. For a moment she thought about leaving that morning but quickly changed her mind to see what was going on. *Given a chance, I would like to present my point of view,* she decided.

She had breakfast with everybody else the next morning. Kareem looked quite cheerful. Fateema has come to her senses, he thought. But Ammiji's eyes bored into her. Once Kareem and Anwar left the room, she asked Fateema to join her in her bedroom.

"Is this what we had asked you to say? Remember, we are taking you to today's meeting so that the young men realize there are educated women with us. Don't wag your tongue.

We want people to see that an inconsequential woman can achieve so much."

Fateema heard her out. So, she was an 'inconsequential woman' to them, a respectable cover behind which they could do what they liked.

The Navapur mijlas was late in the evening one day. No moulvi had been called, but a lecture recorded in a mosque in Britain was played. After that, Kareem stood up. He gave an impassioned speech about Mahmud of Ghazni and Babar, and Mughal rule. The young men listened to him with a glow on their faces. Kareem went back to his seat: a war had been won.

Before Ammiji and Anwar knew what was happening, Fateema took the microphone.

"Brothers, I wish to add to what Kareembhai said. History tells us there wasn't one but many Mahmud Ghaznis. How? It's like this: many communities in the Middle Ages lived a life of plunder and bloodshed. Such plunderers looted merchants and traders in many countries. The ones who came to this country in the name of Islam simply intended to plunder."

The microphone was taken away from her and she was made to sit down, almost by force. Anwar spoke up, "What Fateemaji *meant* to say is that Islam means 'refuge in Allah,' but that those who do not believe in Islam must be fought against."

The evening was brought to an end. Droves of young men circled around Kareem, some came to Fateema as well.

They greeted her politely but kept their distance. One of them, who appeared to be the leader, said to her, "Fateemaji, I agree with you. We need to understand that every age has a different way of living."

"Thank you. Your name?"

"Shamsu."

"What do you do?"

"I just finished twelfth grade. I may now join a Polytechnic."

"That's great. You should do a degree course after your diploma, okay? Your progress will help the quam progress."

"You are so right."

"You will ruin everything we have built, girl."

"Ammiji," Anwar intervened.

It was a post-dinner conversation, out on the lawns. This was their last night together. Ammiji was to leave the following morning. Anwar and Kareem were to return to the crowded, squalid mohalla.

Although Fateema had made up her mind, she tried to mollify Kareem saying, "I don't understand what you want to say. What was wrong with what I said? Shouldn't the quam also progress?"

"Yes, there are different paths of progress though. You better listen to the cassettes and understand. I also have recordings of this last meeting. Listen to Kareembhai properly."

"Do give them to me."

"All right. In any case, let's go in, this place is full of mosquitoes." Ammiji stood up.

Were mosquitoes more terrifying than AK47s? Fateema was amused. If Kareem had remained Kareem they would have had a laugh together. *Do you remember, Kareem, how we fell about laughing when Baapu kept trying to pump up that punctured tyre? Perhaps he does not remember all that.*

They all went into Ammiji's room. Ammiji opened her suitcase and selected a few cassettes to give Fateema.

"Listen to Moulvji and Kareem, and then listen to your own speech: you will know the difference. Now go."

"Thanks."

"Say 'shukriya,' not thanks."

"Jee, shukriya."

Fateema woke early the next day. She got ready and wrote a note to Anwar:

Anwarji, I am sorry to say that Kareembhai and I think differently. Like you, even I want to work for my community and religion. But our paths are different. Khuda Hafiz.

She paused, why was she writing to Anwar? Was he even related to her?

Fateema crumpled up the note and threw it into the wastepaper basket. Was Kareem awake? She wrote a note for him.

My dear brother Kareem,

I am leaving so as to finish my studies. I will continue to stay in a hostel. Kareem, I know my religion well. It is the religion of Allah, not Mullah. Bhai, please quit these people's company. This is a dangerous game to play. There's still time. And don't come to take me back. This is a free nation. I have fundamental rights. For God's sake, finish your education.

Fateema

Without meeting a soul, Fateema left.

A month went by. There was no news of Kareem. Fateema had begun preparing for her examinations. She referred to the books in the library and prepared a comprehensive article for Professor Dilip Shah.

One evening, as she was returning to the hostel after tuitions her eyes fell upon the evening news. Her feet froze and her head began to spin.

"Conspiracy to spread communal tension in the city exposed. Accused absconding."

She bought the newspaper. Her blood froze in her veins. "A guesthouse on the outskirts of the city was raided by the police. The accused had incited the youth and children through meetings and poured poison into their minds. The police have taken a few young men into custody and have begun investigations."

She had feared that Kareem would get embroiled in something like this, but she was implicated, too.

Fateema reached the hostel.

"Traitor! Namakharam!" Manuben spat fire. "Get out of here."

＊

Years had gone by since she heard those words from Manuben. They continued to echo in her ears. This did not mean she will ever forget Manuben's favours. After knowing the truth, Manuben had given refuge to Fateema. She had inspired Fateema to study. When she took up a job and quit college, she had hugged Manuben and sobbed. It was like Ba's funeral for the second time. Such misery.

She now lived in a dark room at a working women's hostel. She ran a welfare centre for Muslim girls and women. Plain clothes policemen visit the area where she lived. She knew that.

Twenty

Run… Run… the volcano was erupting, spewing red flames and lava. People were fleeing, running. People who had been just sitting in their homes, or sleeping, were all fleeing from the lava as it rushed behind them…

Spectators watched this scene on television with bated breath. While most of them were children, the audience also included elderly women like Munirabi, Hazrabai, Asma and older men, like Kaasamchacha and Munawarchacha.

Kareem's room had turned into a community centre. During her holidays, Fateema showed children DVDs of wildlife and geography. She also taught spoken English as well as drawing and elocution. As they watched the volcano erupt, some of the little children clung to Fateema for reassurance.

"Teacher, is this real?"

"Yes, Zaheer. This does happen. Some countries have mountains like these ones."

Of course, to children who had never set foot outside the mohalla to see even their own country, it was difficult to convey what lava was.

"Will this kind of thing happen here?"

"Na bhai. It will not."

"Sure?"

"Sure."

Zaheer's face relaxed. When her Baapu had brought issues of *National Geographic*, she had managed to learn, hadn't she?

"You are very scared, bhai."

"Me too," Amar said. "I also feel scared."

"Oh come on, there's no need to feel so scared."

Amar fell to thinking. "But it is natural to feel scared, Fateemadidi, no? See, if this kind of thing burns our house, where would we stay?"

Fateema could not answer Amar. She realized that children feared homelessness more than they feared lava.

"There's only one house, after all," Zaheer added. These children knew what it was to be without a home. A communal fire two years ago had burned down their homes, Zaheer's as well as Amar's. For months they had lived in relief camps. Their houses were eventually repaired, and some new ones had come up.

Fateema's little class had considerable political support. Assembly members would make provisions for special classes for weak students by paying expenses from their personal fund and also arrange for classrooms in municipal schools. Hindu organizations provided food and books. Women doing zari work or selling vegetables also received loans from Muslim organizations.

Every eye was on the vote bank in this locality, Fateema had no doubt about that.

Fateema was a lecturer in History, a post she took up when Professor Shah retired.

She lived in the working women's hostel. She could have benefitted had she been willing to take the help of Muslim or Hindu organizations. But she preferred to remain Allah's person, or *Allah naa maanah*, as Ba would say. No labels attached. She was paying a price for that choice. But she was proud – nay, heady – about living life on her own terms.

She had not been able to find a house in this city. The builders were cunning, or scared, or simply wary of social disapproval. More than Fateema, it was the men from her community that they were scared of. They would not be able to sell other houses if they gave her one, it was an economic miscalculation, right? Fateema understood why their homes were so dear to the children she taught.

"Fateemadidi, where is your home?" Every once in a while a child would ask.

"Mine?"

"I know, I know. Fateemadidi's house must be in a tall building, the kind they show in films," Amar said.

"Really? How do you go upstairs then?"

"In a lift, Zaheer. I will take you all in an elevator, okay?"

The children left to go home. Fateema knew she had no home to return to, upstairs or downstairs. She told herself this was how things are today, but who's to say they will not change tomorrow? After all, she was the one who taught hope to the women and children she was tutoring.

It was a different matter that she did not use words such as 'message of hope' in her class. She talked to them in their own language. They didn't know that she had a Masters and a Doctorate. Would that have made a difference? Not really.

Fateema had begun this work as a tiny intervention that she would make in the two fields of education and livelihood. She had managed to persuade girls dropping out after the ninth grade to finish their matriculation. She had helped such girls obtain diplomas in teachers' training and do short courses. Uneducated women could now look at possibilities of earning through tailoring, doing henna designs and working in beauty salons.

Help had been forthcoming. Besides politicians, even ordinary people had been helpful.

After class, Fateema left to go to back to the hostel. Amar's words about her non-existent home haunted her.

While she stood waiting to issue books from the library, she heard the librarian talking to somebody about a building project. She heard the name as well.

Fateema's two-wheeler turned in that direction. *Let's see, you never know... No, no it was best not to have high hopes, but still...*

The construction was in full swing even on a scorching summer's day. Without any protection over their heads, masons were busy climbing and putting up scaffolding. Little children rolled on sand pits, covered overhead by their mother's torn saris. Fateema's heart went out to them. She went up to the labourers, thinking that the children ought to be going to a school of some kind. But the workers did not understand her language. It was very hot. She meant to go straight to the builder's office, but she stood rooted to the ground, wiping the sweat off her forehead. She glanced towards the builder's office. She was being examined by the man sitting there.

A bell rang announcing a lunch break. Fateema took a couple of steps towards the office, but stopped again.

Two of the workers washed their hands and feet, then they spread a mat on the ground and folded their legs.

Namaaz! They were praying to Allah for the beautiful world He had created. Something she had read played out before her eyes.

The Prophet had settled in Medina after quitting Mecca.

He entered the city riding a camel. People thronged to stop him, and shouted, "Stop Paigambar, stop here." But the Prophet replied, "I will stop where my camel does." Where the camel stopped became the first mosque established by the Prophet. He also built two small houses. He brought together his relatives, family, well-wishers, supporters of Islam and people who had migrated with him, all bound together by the same faith now. He then climbed on a pedestal with his back towards them and raised his voice to say, "Allah Ho Akbar."

Everybody else joined him by echoing the same words. The Prophet got down from the pedestal. He sat on his haunches and touched his head to the ground three times, surrendering himself to Allah. He asked everybody else to do the same. This is what namaaz is – to touch the head three times to the ground as a prayer to Allah and a complete surrender. That's how namaaz is done even today.

The workers had not missed their namaaz even in such murderous heat? Fateema felt like she was melting. She also sat down.

Then, she straightened her clothes and walked over to the builder's office. The man she had seen earlier sitting outside now sat on a chair behind a small table.

"Excuse me please?"

He looked up, reluctantly.

"What kind of flats do you have in this building?"

"What do you mean?"

"I wish to buy a one-bedroom apartment. Can I see your plans, please?"

"There's nothing here. You may leave."

"Sorry? You build homes to sell, right?"

"We haven't begun anything, so leave."

"How is that possible? One of my acquaintances has booked an apartment here and signed a deal. He is the one who gave me the address."

She had spoken a half-truth.

"I see... okay. But the sheth is not here."

"I can still see the plans can't I?"

"Woman, you're very stubborn. Just let it go," he said, irritated.

"The plans must be in this drawer," Fateema said calmly and stood up. The fellow's cellphone buzzed. He walked out as he talked and Fateema's eyes rested on the drawer. She was tempted to open it to check if one-bedroom apartments were available and for how much.

But she couldn't bring herself to. Meanwhile the fellow, or the manager, came back. He looked at Fateema, and said, "That was my boss. Look, there's nothing to be done right now. So just go." Softening a little, he added, "We are still only making pillars and building a foundation."

"Really? It's already two storeys high, so how is this still a 'foundation?'"

The manager sat down, sipped some water and asked, "Who sent you here?"

Fateema did not want to do a tit-for-tat. After all, she was the one who needed him. With self-restraint and consideration for the one who had sent her, she said, "Surely, when you construct a building, that is public knowledge, right? People like me, who are looking to buy, they get to know about it..."

Her politeness was like water off a duck's back. His voice was laden with scorn and contempt. "We don't sell homes to any old passerby. And by the way, what were you doing with the workers there?"

"Nothing, why?"

"Nothing? You were watching them do namaaz. Is that nothing?"

"Yes. So?"

"You are also…"he stopped. "Have you come to investigate how we treat our workers? Someone else was also here asking why there are no schools for these children. Are we running a charity here? Everything is according to the law. Leave now."

She replied calmly, using the familiar 'you.' "Don't say anything more. You don't look good. What charity are you going to do? Look at your arrogance despite a paltry salary. You sound awful." Fateema left the room.

She was glad to have spoken like Ba in a straightforward dialect. Ba had spoken through her.

Fateema kickstarted her two-wheeler and turned towards the hostel.

She lay on the bed in her room, gazing at the ceiling. The heat inside and heat outside, everything here was 'according to the law' too.

"Law." She knew what law was, but she did not know what it was to be in its clutches. She knew who the police were, but not how it felt to have their tentacles around you.

She did get to know, and along with that, the true colours of many other people.

She turned on her side and stared at the faded wall where images played out as though on a screen.

"Traitor! Namakharam! I gave you refuge in the hostel thinking you were a good woman; and this is what you did! Don't you dare step into this place!"

Manuben's hot flaming words.

The police were looking for her. They had come to the

hostel, and were questioning Manuben instead: Where? When? Who had come to meet her? Did she tell you anything? Any telephone numbers?

Of course Manuben mentioned that she had come through a school run by their Trust. She's a good girl. She'd never do anything like that.

But to Fateema she said, "I said good things because you are a girl. I didn't want the police to make mincemeat out of you. Traitor."

Me? A traitor? Arre, I was the one singing the national anthem on Independence Day every year!

What had happened? How did it happen? The police had warned Manuben: Let her stay on here. We can get in touch with her that way.

She had no choice, she was made to stay in the hostel.

She had realized the terrorist sides to Ammiji and Anwar, which is why she had left after writing the letter. The two of them, along with Kareem, had gone underground.

Fateema sat by the hostel window and wondered if Kareem was with Ammiji and Anwar. She would usually sit by the window and look at the sky. Today, though, her eyes stopped at the window bars.

The truth spread through her body like venom. The police would now question her. They must be on their way already. She had read the memoirs of a British woman arrested on charges of collaborating with insurgents. Was she going to prison? She shivered at the thought.

She was summoned to the police station.

An empty room, except for two wooden chairs and a table.

Sit down. Your name?

Fateema Lokhandwala.

What do you do?

I am an M.A. student. I live in the college hostel.

Are you a student or a lecturer in communal tensions?

I have not given any inflammatory speeches.

Liar, bloody wh–! We have witnesses who have heard your speeches.

He was perched on the table and yelling at Fateema.

Call your witnesses and ask them to testify in my presence.

Kareem is your brother?

Yes.

Older or younger?

Older.

What does he do?

He was… is studying.

Where is he now?

I don't know.

You don't know. You live with terrorists for five days and you don't know?

Third day in the lock-up. Fateema had juvenile delinquent girls for company, thieves, mothers-in-law who had torched their daughters-in-law, women involved in body trafficking. They were dragged into the prison cell in the evenings. During the day they were allowed to move around in the open compound. Ramjabai ruled this universe. Jailor and warden. *Be scared of her*, a rake-thin co-prisoner whispered into Fateema's ears.

Ramjabai pulled her thick braid violently and pushed her, "Oye, why're you here?"

Fateema did not reply. She tried to shrug off the hand clamped on her hair but it was not easy. A woman constable stood at some distance. Ramjabai let Fateema go. "Listen, no crying here, understand? This is your home now."

So this prison is now my home? Fateema looked up to ask Allah.

Twenty-one

Clad in a white sari with a colourful border, Fateema sat on the floor, shrinking and retreating into herself. Her dupatta had been taken away by the lady constable lest she use it as a noose and hang herself. In exchange, she'd been given a sari. The white blouse was big enough for at least two Fateemas to fit in. Who must have worn this earlier, she wondered. Something was poking into her. She groped to find three ants and squashed them with her fingers. They'd come back at night. Such was life in a prison cell.

This is my home, from now on.

The sky and the neem tree looked bent beyond the window. Her home in the village, the neem tree, a restless Ba – all of them seem to bend at this moment.

"Why are you here, hanh?" said the warden handing over a cup of morning tea. Her next question was in Gujarati: "Did your husband in or what?" Without waiting for Fateema's reply, she continued, "That's what the rascals deserve, you should have seen mine. I did all the work, carried his seed in my stomach and he brought a whore. I was so furious… I hit him with a hammer… I am Manki, not one to take shit, I tell you."

"You… are a prisoner?"

"For ten years," Manki replied.

"Ten years? You've been here?"

"Now they have made me a warden because of my good behaviour. This is where I live, and work. This is my home now."

Fateema downed the tea. Her head reeled. This is my home then... my neighbours such as Ramja, Sirpa, Kamli.

Her mind and body felt numb. The sounds of chai being served echoed around her. Manki spat out some more expletives as she got up. She asked, "*Case chaale chhe*? Hire a good lawyer. My lawyer got my sentence reduced from twelve years to ten and eventually seven. You can be released on bail, you know. See if someone can do the running around for you."

With this, She picked up the kettle and left.

Blood coursed through Fateema's veins again. A numbness gave way to thoughts of 'bail,' 'lawyer' and 'court.' These words pointed in the direction of freedom.

Ramja stood near a window. The cells were left open for inmates to bathe and clean up.

"Oye... you want?" Ramja asked.

Fateema came to the window and asked, "What?"

Ramja laughed sheepishly and took out a small bundle of tobacco hidden inside her blouse.

"It's tobacco. Do you want some?"

"No... no."

"Okay, okay. It's not very pricey. One rupee a shot."

Fateema turned her face away.

This conversation once again plunged her into despair. An M.A. scholar called Fateema had to be lumped as a criminal along with these women?

Arre, I read about human progress and civilization, I read histories of the rise and fall of empires... I prepare the 'Journals of Fateema' to remember the chronology of historical episodes... and I am stuck in here?

She was ready to collapse into a heap, but instead took courage and touched her head to the ground. *Allah.*

This was the fourth day of the police cross-examination. The room was hot. Fateema had not been given even a glass of water to drink. Manki had been made to sit at a distance in lieu of a woman constable.

Fateema had mentioned all the facts in the very first two days. But she was being asked the same questions again and again, albeit in different words. Some cops terrorized her.

I have told you whatever I know. Now you need to investigate.

Saa...li bitch! If I had your brother with me, I would have beaten him to pulp to get the truth out.

Bai, you are an educated woman, aren't you ashamed of being a traitor to your country?

"Gohil Saheb, you take it easy. Drink some tea, I'll handle this woman." Gohil moved away spitting fire from his eyes.

"Okay, you also drink tea."

"All right." A period of calm, followed by some more questions.

It was an empty room. She saw a Gujarati newspaper on the table. She had not read the paper in four days. Fateema picked it up and scanned the pages.

The world had not changed. She had been thrown into a cell, but no one seemed to have taken notice. How come the police had not publicized her arrest? The headlines on the first page, bits and pieces about scuffles, thefts and robberies, the gimmicks of film stars, deep essays on religion and value... the same old things.

She turned around. Manki was asleep. Poor thing. The ants must have bitten her all night. Fateema finished reading the newspaper. She put it back on the table and sat on the chair. There was hectic movement in the corridor outside.

She would ask them today about a lawyer and the possibilities of bail. If such illiterate and hammer-wielding women knew their rights, why shouldn't she?

They entered the room. Gohil left to go out once again. A series of questions ensued.

"Listen woman, we have searched your hostel room. We did not find anything suspicious there. I am telling you for your own good. You be truthful to us about anything you've been hiding."

"Hiding what?"

"Bloody liar! You were staying with your loved ones, giving speeches and all, and now such drama?" The cop had switched over to the familiar 'you.' He may descend to blows now, but what could she do?

"I am not hiding anything! Whatever I know, I have already told you."

"Haraam…" He stopped himself. Fateema's eyes bored into him.

She spoke in a steady voice: "Mr Joshi, you are a Brahmin. Talk like a Brahmin. Speak with respect to a woman."

Joshi was taken aback. His eyes went to the name-badge on his uniform. "Where are you from? Uttar Pradesh? Bihar? Aazamgarh?"

"You will know all that from my background check, Sir. I am from this place. From a village, nearby. I have studied with the daughters of Brahmins and Baniyas. My gurus were— I mean are— people like Jani Sir, Gaekwad Sir and Professor Dave."

"Hmm," Joshi took a deep breath. He looked uncertain and ordered some tea and biscuits.

Fateema's letter of appeal lay on the table.

Joshi leafed through it. He asked pointed questions about Ammiji and Anwar. Try and remember, some indication, some sign. They have a haveli in Lucknow. They had come here to look for a science teacher.

"Nonsense. They must have come to recruit young men for terrorist camps running in Pakistan. What about your brother? Where would he be? When did you first meet Ammiji?"

"I don't know about my brother. My mother is almost an invalid, living at Aalamchacha's place in the village."

"I know. We went there. Your brother has not been back in years. When did Ammiji return from London? And that cassette with a moulvi's speech, who brought that?"

"I don't know. You can understand, Saheb. I am alone, poor, a woman and a Muslim. My brother has been unable to spot religious fundamentalists."

No, she didn't say this.

Now what? Back to jail? She should ask for a lawyer, but where would the money come from?

Gohil entered the room holding a file. Inside were copies of the police reports and Fateema's letter.

"Take a look at this."

Fateema read through the file and investigation reports. "Is anything missing?"

"No."

"Sure?"

"Yes."

"Sign here." D.S.P. Gohil thrust a pen in her hand. She hesitated. These were legal papers. She didn't know if they were going to lead her into a legal labyrinth.

"Are you waiting for your lawyer?" Gohil said. "No problem."

"My lawyer?"

"Well, you seem to have good friends. We didn't know that. You have been helped by the Hindu Youth organization."

"Hindu Youth organization?"

"Yes, a couple of Muslim men also offered to hire a lawyer for you. But you are free now. You can go. If needed, you will be summoned to the police station. Don't leave the city to go anywhere."

A lawyer in a black coat came in. His name was Jayantibhai Shah. He advised Fateema to sign the papers, which she did.

"As I said, you are free to go. There is no police case against you. We did not find anything objectionable in our investigation," the inspector clarified.

"My client is a respected scholar. The police have been wise to withdraw all charges against her," said the lawyer, pompously.

"Fateema, you are free now. You can resume your education and move about freely." The policeman matched the lawyer with equally pretentious Gujarati.

"That's it? It's over?" Fateema asked in a broken voice. Freedom had come to her with such suddenness.

"That's it." The voice of authority.

She stood up. So did Manki. She had to pick up her belongings from the jail. The lawyer had orders to take Fateema away.

Once the formalities were over and Fateema stood outside the jail, she asked, "Mr Shah, who hired you?"

"Naveen Shukla. Tushar Jani. They were your seniors in school."

"But…." Fateema didn't know what to say. Yes, they were

indeed her seniors. But so what? Why would they come forward to help someone tagged as a terrorist? There was no point in discussing this. Was being a schoolmate enough reason? Or was there something else behind this? It wasn't clear at this moment.

For now, it was necessary to go to the hostel and pick up her belongings from her room.

Jayantibhai said to her, "Ben, it's neither the organization nor me, but you yourself who are responsible for your own release. The credit goes to you, really speaking."

"How? I don't understand."

"In the course of their investigation, the police found cassettes with your speeches on them. They did not incite communal violence."

Of course. Fateema remembered the fury on Ammiji's and Anwar's faces. The microphone had been snatched away from her.

"I told them that."

"The police traced all your movements and that led them to the guesthouse. It was full of your fingerprints."

"Obviously. I had stayed there."

"They found the letter you had written to Anwar in a rubbish bin. They found proof of your distance from them. Although one thing…"

"What one thing?"

"Well, it could be read as a strategy to mislead the police."

"Oh no!"

"Oh yes, Fateemaben, the police knows how terrorists work."

The strong sun shone down. Fateema stood in the shade of a tree. Her legs were shaky. She saw cycles, rickshaws, cars – all speeding away. They had speed and direction. Where was

Fateema to go? Would Manuben return her belongings and slam the door shut?

How could she who had saved Komal, walk into such a trap?

"Ben, you don't look well. Why don't you rest for a bit?"

"Where?" The question rose and fell in her mind.

"All right then, I'll take your leave."

"Wh… what about your fees?" Fateema asked with considerable difficulty.

"No need. Tusharbhai is a builder. He puts a lot of business my way."

The lawyer took two steps forward, but then came back to her.

"Ben, do watch your back."

"What do you mean?"

"The people accused in your case are still free – your brother being one of them. One reason they let you go is to see if you will be contacted by them. I have no proof of this, but it's worth keeping in mind."

Fateema wiped her face with the end of her dupatta. She was convinced. There was nothing more to say. "Take care." The lawyer got into an auto rickshaw and left.

Where was she to go?

She could go to Ba. That house would not kick her out. She could rest her head in Ba's lap and let her tears fall. If only she had gone back to the village after her BA and taken up a job there she could have spared herself all this humiliation. She was paying a price for Baapu's dreams and her own ambitions. Waves of thought and memory crashed over her, pulling her this way and that. Her head bobbed up and down, keeping itself on top of water. She checked her purse: twenty-five rupees. Enough for an auto.

"Traitor!" "Namakharaam!" Did Manuben actually say those words? Why does it seem a long long time ago? Fateema entered the hostel building. *Since when were there security guards at the gate? It was enough to have an old peon, mostly absent, earlier. Arre, there was an intercom as well!*

"ID proof," she was asked in an authoritative voice.

"Sorry, I don't have a card, but you can talk to Manuben."

"Why don't you have a card?"

"This is an intercom, right? Why don't you just call up the administration office, bhai! I told you I don't have a card, why do you keep asking then?"

The guard scowled as he dialled the number.

"Go upstairs. Manuben said you can go in."

Fateema entered her room and slumped on the bed. The police search had left her room in a mess. Not even her notes and reference books had been spared.

Manuben stopped by. She stood at the door, and held out a glass of water to Fateema. "Here, drink this. It's scorching outside."

Fateema stood up and drank the water. She stood staring at the books strewn about her.

"The police did that."

"Of course they must have done, Manuben. They have to catch people spreading venom in society and holding the country to ransom. They have to carry out their investigations." Fateema picked up the remnants of her belongings.

"You were not harassed, I hope?" Manuben didn't have to be specific.

"No, except for the cross-examination, they didn't do anything to me."

"All right. Clear up the mess in your room. And you can continue staying here, Patel Saheb has given you permission."

Fateema was surprised. She had assumed she would have to pack up and leave. Instead she could stay in this room. She looked at the piece of sky from her window and thanked Allah.

She rearranged her books. So, back to college from tomorrow?

Fateema shied away from people's glances. She did not have many regular classes. She preferred to go to the library. Rachel put her arm around her, "I don't want to know anything. Our ancestors were the same centuries ago. We are sisters."

Some days later, as she was coming out of the library, she met Naveen.

"Namaste, Fateema! Do you recognize me? We went to the same school."

"Oh yes… Of course."

This was the Naveen who had helped to get her released.

"Fateema, we run an organization for the unity of young Hindus. We are not into inter-religious hatred at all. Patel Saheb, from your hostel, is our chairman. We would like your support as well. We want to show people that we have religious harmony."

Fateema was dumbfounded!

Twenty-two

How do we understand this many-coloured miracle called the universe?

It was not only her books, Fateema's very life lay scattered around her. Pages with her past moments, years and days lay in pieces. They needed to be picked up one by one, made sense of and ordered. This is what Fateema tried to do every single day. Images of past incidents flickered before her eyes, and Fateema found herself back in that school far away in the village.

Smitaben taught Gujarati prose and poetry in the tenth standard. The line, "How do we understand…" from Umashankar Joshi's poetry would be discussed in multiple ways.

"There is no one formula for interpreting life," Smitaben would say. "Who knows what drives human life, which emotions, intentions and oceans lie beneath us, producing both gems and volcanoes?" Then she stopped, "Arre, you are so young and child-like. Take each day as it comes."

That's exactly what Fateema was doing. She was in prison some days ago. She had a little window there. The tiny piece of sky she saw from that window made her restless for freedom. She was now in a room once again looking outside through a window. She would make her journey outside this room, for this was still not her 'home.' Home was where she and Ba would live.

Husband – a home without a partner?

Fateema shut her eyes and imagined a man. But no image appeared before her eyes. Had she married Anwar... but that was not to be. A woman with a conscience inside Fateema had warned her and rescued her. Never mind. *A many-coloured miracle* – maybe she would still meet someone. Words like 'aashiq,' 'khanvid,' 'mohabbat' from the film songs that Komal sang danced before Fateema's eyes.

She had to summon up all her courage now, and attend classes. Would everyone know? *They will all look at me, move away from me...*

A plainclothes policeman had turned up at the hostel once. Fateema had to go back to the police station for signing some papers, he said.

She reached at the appointed hour. Gohil Saheb had gone somewhere, so Fateema sat in the office waiting for him. She heard someone behind her.

"Fateemabai?"

She turned around and saw Manki.

"Look, you're back again! How are you?"

"I'm fine. Have you brought a female prisoner here?"

"Something like that. That's my *duty* these days." Fateema noticed how she had emphasized 'duty,' like Ba who consciously tried to say 's' instead of her customary 'h'!

"They've taken her inside, this woman. You know she was selling her daughter," Manki whispered. "Isn't the big sahib here to see you?"

"No, he must be on his way," Fateema answered.

Manki suppressed her amusement by covering her mouth with an end of her sari. "Oh, Fateemabai, all this is a drama, you know!"

"What do you mean?"

"You remember once I had brought you here and they had left you alone. The two of us sat here and chatted, remember?"

"Yes."

"They hadn't gone anywhere. There's a hidden camera here. The saheb watches it on the TV over there in his room. He'll see what you do when you are by yourself. They bring a daaktar also sometimes. He can make out from the way people sit or stand whether someone is a criminal. You must have been asked to sit here for the same reason. Chalo, chalo, I don't want to watched on the TV!" Manki fled.

Okay. So they call a psychiatrist, and they must be watching the body movements of an accused in the interrogation room.

She continued to sit there. After ten minutes, Gohil Saheb's assistant came over to her. "Saheb will be some time, he's been held up. You may leave if you want to, but be sure to be present when you are called next time."

"Thank you."

Fateema stood up and left. She was blinded by the sun outside. The rays illuminated her from within. A cloud lifted. She had not committed a crime, what was she scared about?

She resumed her classes from the following day – and was pleasantly surprised that everyone's behaviour towards her was normal. Nobody asked her anything. The police must have carried out the investigation in a covert manner, she thought, perhaps so that she could be proved innocent, sent back to her college and watched for future purposes.

Or was this part of Patel Saheb's strategy for the upcoming elections? Take it as it comes. She had to study, that's all.

People have short memories. Fateema crumpled the unpleasant memories into a ball and threw them away. She plunged back into reading once more.

A police jeep appeared yet again. It stood at some distance from the college. A woman constable got out, dressed in plain clothes. Fateema was taken to Kareem's room. The same open drains, crowded homes and squalor. The police began questioning her once they were inside Kareem's room. They searched his suitcase, utensils: nothing. The walls were scratched to check – for a number, a sign, something. Fateema's eyes filled with tears at the thought of Kareem's disappearance as well as her own idiocy. Arre, she should have simply phoned the police then.

They took her to the guesthouse again. She knew about her fingerprints there, along with those of Ammiji, Kareem and Anwar. During the police investigation it was established that the bungalow was rented by a Non-Resident Indian. Along with the bungalow came a cook and gardener. Fateema was made to accompany the police to all the places where meetings were held. She was wrung like a piece of cloth to get answers out. She was also shown sketches of Ammiji, Anwar and Kareem. Finally, this too ended, and they let her return to college.

There was a seminar on Gandhian ideology at college. As usual, Professor Dilipbhai asked her to prepare something.

Fateema went to Gujari bazaar with Manuben. Manuben muttered that it was a waste of time looking for books, but she accompanied her anyway. While Manuben rummaged through old photoframes, Fateema looked through the books. Her eyes fell upon bound volumes of an old journal. She was stunned to see the dates. They were published in 1861 by a Parsi press!

Excitement coursed through her. She stowed the journals in her dupatta and paid the price immediately without haggling. She guarded the books like hidden treasure. She began reading what she had on Gandhi. She also had a collection of his lectures given during the Dandi March.

Her eyes came to rest upon a paragraph in an article by Gandhi dated 27th April, 1930:

> Swaraj is neither for Hindus nor Muslims alone. It is for everybody. One can't expect anything different from a Satyagrahi. We are not to get rid of anyone. We are leaves of the same tree…

Another article carried a description of the Dandi March:

> Gandhiji walked through Paldi in Ahmedabad and set foot on the banks of the river Sabarmati. Thousands of mill-workers joined him in this holy pilgrimage. Where four people could have been imagined, thousands fitted into that space, protesting against unfair laws, and foreign repression with a pinch of salt…"

Fateema continued to read. History came alive before her eyes. What times were those when Hindus, Muslims, Christians, Brahmins and non-Brahmins rubbed shoulders with each other to create a new world! And yet nobody carried a single weapon! Non-violence was their weapon, of course.

In one of Gandhi's speeches he said, "I have heard complaints that when police or government officials seek food or water, it is not given to them. Our religions do not teach us to starve people to death, regardless of whether they are natives or white. Gripped by the same religion, I have set out from home…"

Where did Gandhi draw his strength from?

Fateema found references to many small episodes in the lives of Gandhi and Kasturba – for instance, their refusal to step into a temple that denied entry to lower castes. However, Kasturba did go for darshan to one such temple (Jagannathpuri?) and incurred Gandhi's wrath. Baapu admitted that he had been a heartless husband.

Fateema wrote an essay covering many such facets of Gandhi's life and gave it to Professor Shah. He was very pleased. "All this will be useful for your Ph.D. should you wish to do that after your Masters," he said.

Such words helped chart a new direction. She knew, though, that she couldn't survive simply on a meagre scholarship and a couple of tuitions. Sooner rather than later, she needed to get herself a job. If nothing else, she needed to earn enough to provide Ba a life of rest and respect.

There was little point relying on Kareem. Had she known this before, she would not have relied on him at all even in the past. Did Ba know about Kareem? The police had most definitely gone there. Honestly speaking, Fateema should have visited Ba as soon as she was free of the clutches of law, but she dreaded doing that. If Ba and she were together, Kareem might try to contact them, and that's exactly what the police wanted. They would have nabbed Kareem the Terrorist.

Shouldn't Fateema have gone to Ba to let her know that?

What had these last few years done to Ba!

Fateema's tears flowed as she hugged her mother. The loneliness of hostel life and the recent hardships had all but crushed her.

Ba's limbs had gone limp due to arthritis. She had had cataract surgery in her eyes, so they were fine, but her body had withered. She had mostly been staying at Aalamchacha's house.

Fateema cleaned the house. The walls had cracks in them. The floor that Kareem had had repaired was now dusty. The steps to the front yard were broken. The stone slab under the drinking water and the cupboard doors had also come apart.

"Never mind if they are broken. I don't need to see them for long!" Ba said.

"Ba, once I have finished my studies I am taking you with me."

"Arre, where?"

"Wherever I find work."

"Are you mad? You find yourself a good man and do a nikaah. That would make me happy."

"Inshallah."

"No beti, that's not enough. Look for a good girl for Kareemiyo as well. He will be able to find his kind of girl in the city."

So Ba didn't know.

A dim darkness drew over the house in the evening. Fateema sat on the broken steps. Ba sat on a plastic chair inside. The mother and daughter gazed at the darkness spreading itself into the house. The more invisible the world became, the more open it was somewhere else. Ba began to talk.

"I must have been fifteen or so when I married your father. My father was a hawker. His job was to sharpen knives. Who knew anything about school in those days? Your father was somewhat literate. The kazi asked, do you accept this marriage? So I said, yes. What else was to be done but to accept? Bas, there was this one obsession your father had. My children must study and become sahibs. Never mind if his feet were worn out from constantly riding a bicycle, he would say, my children will drive two-wheelers."

"Ba, forget all that now. You have me, nah?"

"They came here looking for Kareem. I told them, go see if

you can find him. If he was here, would I not have beaten him to a pulp? Is this what he is up to? Is this what your father slogged for?"

"The police…" Fateema couldn't finish.

"Yes, they turned everything upside down. Baapa, you search where you want, I said. Before they left, they warned me: you better report to us when he comes, or else you'll find yourself behind bars."

Fateema was wounded.

"Ba, so much happened and you didn't tell me?"

"Look at you, have you forgotten that I can't write? How do I mention this to anyone? The rascals would have harassed you as well."

Fateema held her head in both hands. Ba did not know much. She must take Ba with her now, even if that meant living in that dirty neighbourhood. She would find herself a part-time job. The following day she said, "Ba, I will manage something as soon as I go. I am not letting you stay here anymore. You come with me."

Ba did not respond. She rearranged her dupatta over her head.

"How can I leave a house behind and come, beti? What if that Kareem fellow turns up?"

"Arre…"

"You forget that Jamaal may return some day. The boys will go back if they see a closed house. If the doors are open, my boys can turn up someday."

This was a mother speaking: she would not shut the doors of her house.

Fateema looked for a part-time job as soon as she was back. A silver lining appeared on the horizon.

"Fateema, I am close to retirement. But I will definitely put in a word for you. Unfortunately such appointments are made by the government now," Professor Shah said to her.

"I know, Sir. So I thought of looking for a part-time job at least."

"Yes, of course. That's very important. I will let you know as and when I come across something."

Some days later, Rachel said to Fateema: "Someone has come to see you. I have asked him to wait outside."

A surprised Fateema came out of the reading room to find a man sitting on a plastic chair reading a newspaper.

"Fateemaben?"

"Yes."

"Our boss wants to see you. This is his card. Do talk to him and meet him."

He left.

Fateema went to a nearby shop and dialled the number.

"Come and meet us. We have your job application. We need assistance."

When Fateema visited, she was told, "Work for a month. If your English is good, we might be able to provide you with a full-time job."

Her job was to translate, she was informed. Speeches by our leaders had to be translated from Gujarati and Hindi into English. Elections were a year away, but preparations must begin.

Fateema was given the speeches for translation. As she looked through them, a shudder went through her.

Twenty-three

"So, any news about your job application?"

"Yes, Sir. I was called for an interview. The job involves translating political speeches from Gujarati into English."

"Make your terms clear. You never know, these political party types will make you chase them for payment later."

"That situation won't arise. I declined the offer."

Professor Dilip Shah did not respond immediately. "Good decision. I can understand that sometimes such speeches are full of mud-slinging. Don't worry. Something else will turn up."

Fateema became an English tutor. It wasn't sufficient for her to bring Ba, but now it was only a matter of a couple of years. She had to do well in her MA exams. Fateema was ready to give what it took.

One afternoon, Manuben visited her in the library. Rachel brought her over to Fateema. Manuben sat down quietly for a moment.

"Chalo ben, you will have to go to your village."

Fateema's felt her heart hammer. Village? Was Ba sick?

Rachel held her hand, and offered her water. On the way back, Manuben told her, "Ba passed away in her sleep this morning. The doors were open so the neighbours came to know very soon. They called up at the hostel... Good ones go away like this, Ben. Would you like me to come with you? Will you be able to go alone?"

She was alone in the journey of life, what was a bus journey in comparison?

Fateema reached the village that evening. She sobbed as she held Ba's lifeless body. "Ba, I didn't want you to be in this house. But you wanted open doors…"

✳

"Sit, Sahib will be here any minute."

It was winter, but the days were not particularly cool. The whirring of the fan at the police station did nothing to lessen the heat. She had covered her head and arms with a dupatta and simply waited.

In a little while someone called Parmar arrived.

"I am in charge of this place now. Mr. Gohil has been posted elsewhere."

"Jee."

"Listen, there was a reason for calling you. We need to ask you something."

"Yes?"

"Okay, let's get on with it." Parmar took out a file from a drawer. He turned the pages. Suddenly, he looked up and said, "Where's your brother?"

"I don't know."

"Hmm. No letter, or phone call?"

"Nothing."

Parmar did not try to prove her wrong. He kept turning pages and paused to look at some photographs.

"The Indian police has a solid network. We haven't stopped with our investigations. Meanwhile the Delhi police has sent us these pictures. Take a look."

Fateema looked at the first picture. A human body lay in pieces. Another photograph showed only the top half of a body, and a clean-shaven face. Leaving behind an illusory world was a man: Kareem.

Fateema did not tremble. She did not shriek. She fainted.

"Fateemabai, stay for another day."

"Sister, thanks, but no."

"Are you sure you want to leave? Should I check first?"

It was not clear with whom she was going to check. The doctor or the police?

The doctor gave her her discharge papers. She brought them with her to the hostel room. She had bought a sandwich on the way which she ate and then lay down on the bed. It was very quiet. Manuben had gone out. She could hear footsteps going up and down the stairs near her room, but nobody came to her side. She'd had her share of sorrows – they had arrived like rocks rolling down the cliff. Jail, Ba's death, Kareem. She lay lifeless, gagged.

In the afternoon, a security guard gave her an envelope. The flap was open, and the handwriting looked familiar. It was from Kareem.

She unfolded it. There was no address or date. It was as if Kareem was talking to her.

> Fatee, I will not tell you where I am. I know that the police have been after you. We committed the crime, but you got the handcuffs. Once you left, we – Ammiji, Anwar and I - began thinking of how to make you a devout Muslim woman. The night you left, three men from Lucknow arrived. They had to be shown the railway station. I was told, 'Miyan, when the train approaches the station, blow the bridge. Make sure as much is destroyed as possible.'

I said yes. They left. They had drawn the station and bridges on a map. I had learnt to make bombs in Pakistan. But I had not used any. It was clear that the guesthouse had to be vacated. The plan was to make bombs in the garage there. Ammiji repeatedly said, 'Kareem, history tells us that the day the Prophet was born, the palace of the Emperor of Iran quavered, its fourteen minarets collapsed, Zoroashtra's fire was extinguished, and lakes disappeared into the earth. Kareem, the Jews and Christians believe in one God, but Mohammad is their last Prophet. With the Koran in one hand and a sword in the other, we need to spread the message of Islam: jihad.'

Before I could do or say anything, there was a phone call for Ammiji. I didn't know who had called but she had to leave the same night. Every sign of our existence there had to be removed. Ammiji ordered, 'Your sister Fateema is dangerous. She will lead all of us to disaster. Kareem, you are a soldier of Islam. Destroy her. Tomorrow. Then put a bomb at the station and come directly to Lucknow. Khuda Hafiz.'

Jihadi that I was, the following day I sat at the station with bombs in my bag. Three trains had arrived. I had to leave the bag near the railway bridge and press a remote. Once that was done, my plan was to kill you. I had a knife with me.

Fateema, I cannot tell you what happened after that. You are educated, so you will understand. Fatee, I was sitting on a bench at the platform. One of the trains had arrived, and the next one was awaited. I was facing a train that pulled in on the tracks across. It was choked with passengers. Many of them got down. I suddenly saw that Ba was also one among them. Fatee, it was our Ba, the same torn black dupatta, a shabby kurta and salwar. You think I don't know Ba? But how come? I kept looking at her. No sound escaped me.

Ba came towards me. She seemed to look past me. She sat beside me. I froze.

Ba said, 'Rascal, you want to kill your sister?'

Fateema, I heard Ba's voice. It was her. I forgot Ammiji and Anwar. All voices from the mornings of that house in the village came alive. Baapu's broken chain, Jamaal and Saira's giggles, Ba's screams, and Aalamchacha's rooster—all this deafened my ears. I didn't realize that in the midst of that cacophony Ba had left, crossed the tracks and taken a train. By the time I came to my senses, both the trains had gone. The platform was empty. I got up. I came to my room. I had to empty it the next day. I threw the bombs into a lake.

Fateema, I have to tell you this. Inshallah, we may or may not meet again. I will go to the station again tomorrow. Ba will definitely come. I want to tell her, Ba, I wouldn't have killed Fateema. I would have only pulled her ponytail and punched her in the back.

But what if Ba does not come? If she comes to you please tell her that Kareem would have only punched you."

The letter ended. There was no signature. Fateema turned on her side and gazed at the wall. The letter fell from her hands and fluttered to the floor. Tears streamed down her face. The sheet and the pillow were wet. Baapu, Ba, Jamaal, Saira, Kareem… where had everyone gone? She cried herself to sleep and fell into a sort of unconscious state.

She woke up early in the morning. There was no need to get out of bed. Bas, there was nothing to do.

Morning drew in, forcing life upon her. Fateema sat up. The nightmare of the previous night was real. Fateema bent down to pick up Kareem's letter.

After Ba's death she had brought some things back with her from home. Old issues of *National Geographic*, Ba's black dupatta, Saira's red ribbons, Jamaal's marbles, Ba's Holy Koran – to all this, she added the letter from Kareem. The envelope was open. The police must already have read it.

How did Kareem die? Would he have gone to the station the next day? Did he see Ba? He must have crossed the tracks. Ba must have been sitting there. Was he cut to pieces by a moving train? The train that he wanted to blow up blew him up instead? The bag with bombs was found next to him. Did they identify him through his fingerprints?

What was the point of all these questions now? A fortnight later, her tears had dried up. Manuben persuaded and threatened, and finally sent her back to college. She had only one thing to say: If you don't study, you can't stay here. Then where would she go? She didn't have a home. The one far away in the village was of no use to her.

One morning she read a piece of news. Terrorists had bombed the British Consulate building in Pakistan. Thirty people had died. Ammiji and Anwar were in a queue for UK visas. They had also been killed. The headline said: 'Terrorists targeting Gujarat become a target'. The police identified the bodies and confirmed the news.

It was all over. All that was left behind was a bloody episode.

"Fateema, congratulations, you've been selected!" Professor Dilip Shah informed her.

There was a seminar on the history of Gujarat in Junagadh district. Two lecturers and two students were to be selected as delegates. Fateema and Sheela Chaudhary made the grade and Professors Dilip Shah and Dave were also going. A thrill ran through Fateema. She had paid the registration fees as well. In the dark alleys of life, Fateema groped her way along. There were some people who tried to rescue her from loneliness and looked after her. She understood that.

This was her first opportunity to participate in a seminar. All the way to Junagadh, she wondered what kind of students she would meet, she thought about the papers she would get to listen to. Sheela Chaudhary was the daughter of a civil services officer. She had travelled all over the country. But Fateema's excitement infected her as well.

They were given a warm welcome at the station. A bus took them to their destination. Fateema watched the city roll past: it was smaller and much less developed than her own. A delegate from another college stood up and said, "This town is in the cradle of mountains, and the mountains go back to ancient times. If the mountains could speak, we would know how civilization began."

The bus stopped outside a beautiful palace. Its exoticism wore off immediately as they noticed that after Partition, Nawab Saheb's outwardly beautiful palace had turned into a building housing government offices and guest houses. An enormous room was given to the four students to stay in. All the houses in Fateema's lane back in the village could have fitted into that one room. So large!

The balcony overlooked a huge garden. Was this palace a 'home'?

"Arre yaar, have some fun! Until we go back to our hole of a hostel!" Sheela reminded her.

The first session was on figures in history. There was a fair amount of discussion. The first speaker spoke about Emperor Akbar. He said, "Friends, from Hindi films you will know about Saleem and Anarkali and Akbar and Jodha – and you may have applauded their immortal love with a 'Wah, Wah'."

Everyone laughed.

The speaker then went on to enumerate the number of Begums and other women in the harems of Akbar and Salim.

"Several Rajput kings had sworn allegiance to the Sultanate of Delhi, but the King of Mewad, Maharana Pratap, remained unmoved. After battles that lasted more than five months, the Rajputs put up their lives like martyrs. Their wives and daughters gave themselves to death by fire. The Rajputs fought with valour and heroism. So infuriated was Akbar by them that he went on a rampage killing people in Chittorgarh. Thousands of innocents were massacred." A hush fell over the seminar hall.

This was followed by discussions about Gandhi, Jinnah and Nehru, with new light thrown on these leaders by the emerging scholarship on Partition.

Fateema listened to all this with rapt attention, fascinated by the letters, reports, and the different sources that history could use.

The discussion of the first session spilled over into the second. One of the speakers gave an eloquent lecture on the uses of studying the past. He described history as being like a telescope, allowing us to see objects and situations far away. He also talked about how history teaching could be made engaging.

The following day was packed with visits to historical monuments in Junagadh. Some people went off to climb Mount Girnar while the others returned to the guesthouse. The guide brought the delegates to see the Ashoka inscription at the bottom of Girnar. He told them about the bloody war of Kalinga, Ashoka's transformation, his conversion to Buddhism, and how he had left behind his inscriptions in many parts of India. Fateema thought about the history of non-violence and peace ensuing from those developments.

"Chal yaar, aren't you coming up to Girnar?" Sheela asked. Some of the young women had taken walking sticks and were ready to start climbing.

"Yes, of course." Fateema joined in. With walking sticks for support, they climbed through the gentle heat of December.

The higher they got, the cooler it became, and the wind whistled around their ears. Fateema wrapped herself up in a black shawl that Manuben had lent her.

"What is there to see when we get up there?" Fateema asked.

"Exquisite Jain temples with intricate sculptures," someone replied. The women sat down to rest. They came across a sadhu, "*Paani peena hai?*" he asked and without waiting for a response offered them water from an earthen pot. It was soothing. Sheela offered him money, but he joined his hands. "This is our dharma."

After a brief rest, the group resumed climbing. It was crowded at the top. Some of the other delegates waved at them. Everyone took pictures.

"Chalo, let's go inside the temple."

"After a bit," Fateema sat down at the temple entrance. She needed to cool her feet. She rested her head against a pillar.

She looked around. Dark boulders and rocks dating back to the beginning of life on earth perhaps; a mountaintop hiding behind the clouds while the earth was a lush green ocean, monuments and temples that held the fragrance of saffron and sandalwood. Fateema felt herself strewn over the landscape, pieces of her dispersed but also cohering into a new shape, the shape of Fateema.

She stood up. On the earth and mountain made by Allah. In one hand she has the Holy Koran. The notes she had prepared for Dilip Sir came back to her:

"The holy Koran has for thirteen centuries filled…"

Through the Prophet, Allah says,

"Let there be no violence…"

She has in one hand the holy Koran, and in another the holy books and teachings of other religions in India. The earth she stood upon is the land on which the Vedas were recited, Ram, Krishna, Buddha and Mahavir stood here and built glorious traditions, the land that Parsis, Christians, Jews and animistic tribes consider their own. She was the inheritor of this multi-religious legacy.

"Arre Fateema, what are you doing here? Why didn't you come inside? did you fall asleep?"

"No, Sheela, I just woke up."

Twenty-four

It was *her* college, there was not a shadow of doubt about that. She had Kareem next to her when she had first set her foot in this place. She had become Fateema, BA Pass here. All Ba knew was that Fateema had done well, '*haari rite pass thayi*,' mixing up her 's's and 'h's as and when she pleased! She had then given Fateema permission to study whatever it was that Fateema had to study. This is how Fateema had now become a Master of Arts. She had obtained a first class and won a silver medal in History. Professor Dilip Shah was due for retirement. Professor Dave had been appointed in his place as head of department. There was also a vacant position in History for which interviews had begun.

The interview panel had a number of external experts on it. Over two days about eight people had been interviewed. Fateema was last. The experts had been given the resumés of every candidate, highlighting their academic achievements, capabilities and experience. This was only an oral interview.

Fateema entered the room, mumbling to herself, "*Bismillah ar rahma meer rahim.*" Her eyes scanned the panel. Manuben's words echoed in her ears. Sit straight, don't stoop, and look up. You are equal to everybody else. *Yes, that's exactly what I'll do.*

She sat on the chair that was offered. She was confident, but also assailed by some self-doubt. What if she didn't get the job? Of course Professor Shah had been very encouraging. But all these people were strangers. Each of them held a copy of Fateema's file. Her grades from high school to her Masters, the scholarship details etc. An unexpected question in a dry tone came in her direction:

"Miss Fateema, as a student of History, what is your perspective on Jinnah?"

"It's a difficult question. The question about who was responsible for India's partition has been raised time and again. You are probably asking the question in that context. Well, those were the turbulent times of World War II. Secondly, the colonized Indians had been fighting against the British rule for over fifty years. Included in this struggle were both Hindus and Muslims occupying polarized positions. All this contributed to Partition."

"What was Jinnah's role in this?"

"Sir, Jinnah was not sectarian in the complete sense of the term. In fact, he had mentioned in a meeting of the Muslim League held at Lahore in 1924 that 'Swaraj' was synonymous with Hindu-Muslim unity. In fact, foreign rule was able to last for such a long time in India because the Hindus and Muslims lacked unity and mutual trust."

Fateema paused, and then continued: "It's rather unfortunate that in the course of time Jinnah came to demand a separate nation. As to why a different nation – Pakistan – the reasons also go back to the foundations of Islam."

The panel members exchanged glances. One of them asked, "Miss Lokhandwala, you are a Muslim. How do you propose to teach the Mughal period to the students of this college?"

Fateema did not immediately respond. Her voice was clear and confident when she did. "Sir, I am an Indian

Muslim. I know the history. You do not distort historical truths. The Mughal invasion of India reflects the militancy of the medieval era. In her book, *A History of God*, Karen Armstrong suggests we look at this as an imperialist expansion. There was no hesitation in the medieval era for rulers to attack the vulnerable and rob them of their possessions. If we accept this framework, it would not be far-fetched to see how the British Empire, the French, the Dutch were also imperialists."

"Well put. Really nice," one of the panel members said. The rest nodded their heads in agreement.

Fateema was worried if she had appeared to be pontificating while responding to such questions. It was good to see their approving nods, but would the next question be about her association with terrorist activities? Quite possibly. Were she to be asked that question, she couldn't blame them. The police had carried out investigations on her.

"Miss Lokhandwala, you have introduced yourself as 'an Indian Muslim.' What is the significance you wish to communicate through that phrase?"

"I am a Muslim inhabitant of the multi-religious, multicultural, multilingual republic of India is what I want to communicate. Diverse religions, cultural currents and languages are our inheritance. They are also our future."

"Another question in this regard: Do you think Hindu-Muslim unity can be achieved?"

Fateema paused. She must be able to articulate well, with the right emphasis that this response needed.

"Unity is on its way to being achieved. Or rather, the efforts began way back, much earlier than we can date them."

"Meaning?"

"From the time of Emperor Akbar. He spent years fighting

battles, but he was also an astute statesman. Although he was not a man of letters himself, he managed to bring to his court representative heads of all religions. He tried to understand their religions, and in order to create harmony between Hindus and Muslims, he created a new religion – Din-e-Illahi."

"Around 1561 CE, perhaps?"

"Yes. And note that we do not discuss this religion any more. In fact, the creation of Din-e-Illahi was acknowledged and appreciated in 1852 in a Gujarati Parsi monthly magazine called *Jagat Premi*. Here, would you like to see it?"

Fateema opened her bag and took out a tome. It was a bound volume of all the issues published from January 1852 to December 1852.

"Sir, this Gujarati monthly came out five years before the 1857 War of Independence."

The expert panel began reading the two pages on Akbar's approach to different religions. The Gujarati prose, its idiom, and printing was 150 years old and quite fascinating. The writer appeared to be Parsi: his Gujarati had a Parsi touch.

Juggut Paremi
Jaanevaari, 1852
Shehenshah Akbar's creation of 'Illahi' in Hindustan

"This is real history. See how much it tells us about the language and ideology of the writer."

"Where did you find this?"

"In the Sunday market. Some family must have discarded this while emptying out a house."

"Or a library weeding out old stuff!"

The panel members talked among themselves as they leafed through other articles in the magazine. There were various subjects with Parsi-Gujarati titles such as, '*Astree kelavini babad ane Mumbai nee udyogshala.*' ('Women's education and Industries in Bombay').

The interview concluded and Fateema left the room. How much she had prepared for the interview, from ancient to modern India! But the questions went in an altogether different direction. Were they checking out my Muslim mentality? Or were they really interested in the questions they asked? She knew Dilip Sir would ask her to lend him those magazines the following day and of course would promise to return them soon. But who knows whether she would get the job. Never mind, she could always do a Ph.D.

With such thoughts in her mind, Fateema reached the hostel. Manuben treated her to tea. She gave Fateema hope about the appointment.

Should she get the job, Fateema would cease to be a student. She would be a lecturer then. She would not be able to stay in the hostel anymore. This was not something Manuben could bring herself to say.

"You are very exhausted. You should take a break and go visit your home for a few days," Manuben suggested.

"Home?" A shock ran through Fateema's nervous system.

Who was at home? Nobody. Baapu, Kareem, Saira – where was everyone? She put sadness at bay by turning her thoughts to Allah. That's where they all were, in Allah's refuge.

Her home was locked. Aalamchacha had been looking after it. The door had become fragile, it merely barred the entrance. Fateema went to Chacha's house and had a cup of tea. She brought the house key and opened the door. She was assaulted by a foetid odour the moment she stepped in. Covering her nose with a dupatta she made a quick dash inside. She looked for a broom to remove the cobwebs that hung on all sides. She began cleaning the house. Objects, or possessions? Hardly any – except Ba's grindstone, some rags, a broken cot and some magazines with colourful pictures.

And, of course, the banter and play of the four siblings, Ba's toil, and Baapu's labour, mud-baked walls and drops of rain falling through the roof cracks… *these are my belongings. I have these stored inside me in a corner.*

She heard a knock at the door. It was Aalamchacha. A stranger stood next to him.

Chacha seemed purposeful.

"Fateema, beti, you know how bad your Chachi's legs have become. Her eyes have also become weak. We plan to shift to Chachi's village."

"That's a good thing, Chacha! You will be looked after over there. But here, this house?"

"That's what, beti! Do you know this bhaijaan? His father was your teacher."

The gentleman picked up the threads of the conversation and said, "Jani Sir."

"Arre, you are Jani Sir's son… but…"

"I was in Bombay. You know Papa's craze for English. He made me study in Bombay. I used to visit home during the vacations."

Fateema did not know this. Naturally. There was no interaction between the girls and boys in the village. Of course, she knew boys from her school.

"I'm in the building and construction business these days. I'll be buying Aalamchacha's house. If you wish to sell yours…"

Fateema was taken aback. It was an unexpected offer. What if Jamaal were to return?

"There's no hurry. Think about it. It's just that this house may collapse any minute."

"I agree."

"My brother Tushar studied with you in school."

"Oh yes, I remember him."

"He's also a builder. He plans to establish a 'complex.' Baapuji lives with him. You see after the car accident…."

"Oh… I had no idea."

The exchange of news continued. She took Tushar's phone number from his brother. Aalamchacha instructed her to visit in the evening.

She stood next to the broken pillars of the house. She could sell the house, but what if she didn't find a job in the city? She may have only this ramshackle house for shelter. She would have to take up a job in the school. Fateema stood erect. She would buy a house. Her own.

Twenty-five

She received the letter of appointment.

It was the month of June. The days were sultry and suffocating. Fateema felt as if she was running through the first welcome showers of the monsoon, such was the joy coursing through her body. She read the letter. Once. Twice. There would be another interview after two years. There was a recommendation to obtain her Ph.D. salary scale – the hell with it – she got the job. *Bismillah e rehmaan e rahim.*

She rushed to Manuben's office and put the letter in her hand. Manuben read it. Raised her eyes to Fateema's joyous face. How many doubts and reservations she had had when this girl first sought admission! Why does Patel Sir bring all kinds of girls to this hostel? she'd thought. It's so difficult to take care of such girls. And yet God taught her a lesson. This girl was the pride of the hostel. She had saved her – the Warden – from what would have been a stigma on her reputation. And now she was a lecturer.

Manuben felt like a mother who one day looks at her daughter and asks herself, when did this girl grow up? Tears trickled down her cheeks as she looked at Fateema. Fateema's own eyes were also moist.

Every year as the girls left the hostel they would come, one by one, to bid her goodbye. They would weep and in turn would make Manuben weep. Manuben would often say, come together, all of you. It's too much to cry with each one of you individually.

The searing pain of separation she felt today was unprecedented. She rose and walked over to Fateema. It was heartbreaking. She could barely manage a sound. She wiped Fateema's tears. She said what she had to with a heavy heart,

"Do come by sometime."

And she broke down.

As Fateema registered the meaning of her words, she felt as if the earth had slipped from beneath her feet.

From hostel to a working women's hostel. The women who stayed there were independent women who had jobs. Yes, there was an administrator whose sphere was restricted to hostel administration. Fateema was allotted the last room on the first floor. The room was smallish and there was no roommate. The bathroom and toilet were next door.

Leaving the hostel behind diminished the joy of getting a job somewhat. Some afternoons, the lights had to be switched on in the afternoons too. As she lay on her bed and stared at the ceiling, the ceiling moved feebly. She would warn herself then. Self-pity? Arre, no: she can't go down that road. If she got caught in that vortex... She recalled how she had told herself the same thing while staring at the walls of her prison cell but then there was hope for bail. Now...

Such uprootedness. Home, hostel, prison, and now this hostel. Stopping everywhere for a while, and then once again moving on. Kareem's room. How could she have forgotten that?

Gradually her room became her home. Since there was no kitchen she began to use the tiffin service. She conserved all her energy for teaching, her Ph.D. and her young friends at the mohalla. And one day someone said, "Fateemaben, now that you are 'permanent', you are entitled to a loan. Buy a house of your own now."

Her dream stirred again.

"You are giving five per cent of your salary to the working women's hostel. That amount will take care of your loan installments."

"But…"

"What do you mean, but? Even a small house will be *your* house."

And then she left the working women's hostel. She rented a room in a poor locality. Yes, she needed to save up money to make the down payment.

A routine – a strange one – to make inquiries for a house and to hear different answers.

"The plans aren't ready yet."

Two floors of the building were constructed and the builder's representative was calmly making this statement. What could she do? Her eyes went across to the pile of bricks nearby. This much, maybe a few more bricks and I would have a room, kitchen, a small bedroom with a small balcony.

"But how can we allot a flat to a single woman? There's no provision in the society rules…"

"But you have barely finished the bhoomi pujan, how can there be society rules?"

"If they don't exist today, they will be formed tomorrow. Why unnecessarily block your money?"

The speaker seemed so magnanimous, so keen to save Fateema's money.

In the staff room, Niruben, Vinodaben would sometimes make inquiries. But what could they do? Yes, Niruben knew someone, a distant relative or some such. He was a builder. She'd been there, but her experience was the same. Sometimes she was overcome by despair. She was desperate to quit the mohalla where she rented a room – the filth, the noise, the fights between husbands and wives and the daily struggle at the public tap. And yet she felt strangely tied to the place, especially since she had begun to spend a few hours in a week with the local children, and with the young girls who had dropped out of school.

"What is this you are teaching? Teach them religion," she was told a couple of times.

Realizing that her work would be more convincing than words, she would reply gently, "Bhaijaan, how can I teach them religion when I am a learner myself?"

And six months later, when the girls from her mehndi class began to earn money at weddings, she had the satisfaction of hearing, "*Rozgari badi kaam kee cheez hai.*"

Out of the blue, she received a letter from a stranger. She read it with surprise. The address was her house in the village. The postman must have given it to Aalamchacha. She read it again. Who could this be? She didn't recognize the handwriting.

"Fateemaben, you do not know me. How would you? My name is Chandrakant Patel. I live in the United Kingdom. Recently I travelled to Africa and I met someone who knows you. He remembered you. He belonged to your village and knew your younger brother well. He even told me that you used to play a game of catching the moon falling through the cracks of the roof. He liked my name 'Chandrakant.' We became close friends. He wept remembering all of you, your Baapu and Ba. Since we became such close friends I would like you to consider me your younger brother.

Chandrakant Patel"

The letter mystified her. Who was this person? How was

he linked to her family? Her only fear was that somehow the letter was connected to Kareem. What should she do? There seemed to be only one alternative. She burned it.

The mohalla she lived in had had no water supply for the past two days. The gutters overflowed with filth. Piles of waste lay strewn about.

It was insufferable. For two days, she had gone to Manuben's house to bathe. But the struggles of living this day in, day out…

One morning she reached the sanitation office. She tried to argue and reason with the Ward Officer. It was like hitting her head against a stone wall. The officer gave a perfunctory assurance, "Everything will be regularized by tomorrow." On her way to her two-wheeler, she heard someone call out to her, "Fateemaben."

She turned around to find a vaguely familiar face. And then it dawned upon her:

"Tushar?"

"Wow, you recognized me!" He came closer. "Why not though? We were in school together. Fateemaben, my elder brother met you in the village. Why don't you come to my site office this evening? We can talk there." Tushar gave her his visiting card.

Bholenath Builders and Real Estate Agent. She read it again. She was astonished by this twist of fate. By this time Tushar was back in his car, "*Aavjo* then," he said, and left.

She rode along on her two-wheeler back towards college. Arre, all along she had been knocking on the doors of builders, putting up with their dismissive behaviour, hoping that she would find a small refuge for herself. And today a builder had offered his business card to her! Let's see what this is about.

She was reminded of Chandan. Once, Chandan had said,

"Sages in our religion meditate at one place and that's 'tapas,' penance. But our guru says that when human beings carry out their work quietly and ethically, help others and become better human beings, that's also penance. So when you and I study properly, that's all penance, you know?"

Was Fateema's penance bearing fruit now?

In the evening, Fateema went directly to Tushar Jani's site office. It was small and empty. On the wall hung visual projections of the twin buildings under construction. She went closer to take a look. The complex was situated on the end of an L-shaped intersection. A tall seven-storeyed tower was going to be built near the entrance facing the main road. Adjacent to that would be a smaller, four-storey building. When she looked into the distance, she noticed that the smaller building was on its way to being built.

Tushar had arrived. He ordered a soft drink for her. "So Fateemaben, you are now a Professor, hanh?"

"You haven't done badly either! Look at you... such status! Anyway, I have been meaning to meet you, Tushar, for all the help you extended. I wanted to say thanks, but your lawyer wouldn't let me."

Tushar was defensive. "I was very busy, you see, with all this."

"Or didn't you want your association with me to be known? Whatever. Let me thank you now at least."

Tushar did not respond for a moment. Then he said, "You are right. I am not defending myself. We, that is I, Naveen and some others, work for a Hindu youth association. Patel, that is Gaekwad Sir's close friend, is also with us. Had our names appeared as the ones who bailed you out, it would... well, I did explain everything to my lawyer."

"I know. You were very helpful."

"Now forget about all that. First things first. My elder brother met you in the village. We bought Aalambhai's house. But we need more space."

Fateema heard him out, wordlessly. Tushar continued, "Fateemaben, now that you have moved to this city, you don't need that house in the village. In any case you are not likely to live in a house with no amenities. So… I mean…"

"What makes you think that I live in a house with amenities here?

"All right, but at least the houses here would have some comforts, nah?"

"If houses exist, yes."

"I knew that you were in a ladies' hostel. I was going to get your address from the college office, but fortunately I bumped into you."

"Had you procured the address and visited my room, you would have known what comforts I live with! I wouldn't have been knocking about in Municipality offices then!"

"I'm sorry. But surely you can get a loan? Why don't you buy a house?"

Fateema edged closer to Tushar's table and looked him in the eyes, "Would you sell me one?"

Tushar sat up. He could not meet Fateema's eyes.

"You want my place, I want yours," Fateema clarified. She had switched to the familiar 'you' without knowing what gave her the right to. She studied with Tushar, and was perhaps like a sister to him.

"That's right, ben. We are making a small colony that people in our village can afford to buy, the kind that our teachers would be able to buy as well. But look at the land prices in the village and compare them with this city."

"So you want to buy cheap and get away?"

"No, no. That's not what I am saying. I wouldn't dream of doing that. To rob you of your house like that. But these are expensive homes here."

"And yet builders are not ready to sell them. Including yourself." Tushar turned the paperweight over in his hand and remained quiet. Then he spoke. "Your mother looked after my elder sister when she was suffering from cancer. How can I forget that? Fateemaben, can I be honest? You … you belong to another religion. If we sell you a house, we won't be able to sell the rest."

She heard him out. "Arre, Tushar, you think you are saying something new to me? You think I don't know? I have been struggling for four years now! I know why doors close on me."

Tushar smiled wistfully. "Ben, it's like this. Our religions are different, our customs, festivals, celebrations are also different. My clients will run a mile away from the smell of meat. Also we've heard that the sacrificial animal is cut at your homes in the mohallas. Arre, the very thought is frightening. Of course, this happened in our religion also, in the days gone by. Mother goddesses used to be placated with blood. But now everyone lives by reasonable norms. Ben, what can I say? You have been with us, so you know everything."

In her mind's eye, Fateema saw the many evenings she had spent at Chandan's house, standing on the cot and swinging, while reciting Gujarati poems. Chandan's grandmother would finish eating her meals before sunset to avoid *jeevhinsa* – violence to any living being.

"What can I say, Tushar? My house will not have any of this."

"I know. Papa's diary mentions your name so many times."

"Jani Sir's diary? My name?"

"Yes. After his car accident, we left that rented home and came here. Along came the diary. It had many references to school. You had won an elocution prize? Essay competition? Papa had written: *I am proud of her.*"

The same Jani Sir had reprimanded Chandan by saying, "You are eating with a Mussulman!"

"Papa was in a coma after the accident. He would have been so happy to see you so well educated."

"He was the one who began English classes for us."

"Yes," Tushar replied. Then with some hesitation, "That's what, you know. We read the diary, we understood his feelings and arranged for your bail."

No one knows where, but somewhere, a powerhouse is operational. Its wires are connected, and at the opportune moment, the switch appears in our hands. Allah has made all these arrangements.

Yes. If not now, when?

She asked, "Can I see the project blueprint, Tushar?"

Tushar opened a drawer and gave Fateema the construction map.

Would she get a house finally? *Bismillah ar rehmaan mir rahim,* Fateema chanted while taking the plans. This was going to re-map her life. She held the paper tight. Fifth floor, house number four, a tiny balcony.

She put her finger on the house. "Done. This small house is mine. When can I come to discuss the payment and the agreement?"

The deal for the village house was concluded. Tushar prepared the property deeds. Jayant, the lawyer, explained the terms to Fateema, the difference in price, FSI, land price, fittings inside the flat. Fateema had not realized that all this also went into building a house.

Another foundation, a brick, a plinth or whatever you call it was also used.

"Ben, keep the news about buying this house low-key, okay? I won't be able to sell rest of the apartments otherwise," Tushar requested her.

Three months had gone by. She visited his office to sign the agreement. Four storeys had been constructed. The fifth floor was under construction. The elevator had yet to be put and plastering was unfinished as well.

She signed the agreement. Selling the village house had taken care of most of the expense of buying the apartment. Hers was the only signature on the property deed. Tushar said to her, "Ben, you had another brother, right? If he is not found for seven years…"

Fateema was startled.

"Arre, Tushar, I didn't realize that." She told him about the letter she received from Chandrakant Patel.

"You have the letter?"

"No… I burnt it."

"Good. Forget it. Ben, you didn't understand, did you? This Chandrakant Patel is your brother."

"What? What are you saying?"

"Some agent must have provided your brother a passage abroad under the name of Chandrakant Patel. Fake passport of course. He must have been first sent to Africa. Eventually he must have entered the United Kingdom as a businessman from Africa. He writes, 'Consider me your younger brother', doesn't he?"

"Yes! Of course." This news had to sink in. In the short span of her life, sudden revelations had created storms and then settled down to sediment in a little corner of her consciousness. Jamaal is alive. As Chandrakant. So be it.

Tushar gave her a packet of peda to mark the auspicious moment of her signing the deed. "This is good, we don't have to worry about his signature any more. My assistant will show you the building now."

Her aspiration was close to fruition now. She would be seeing her own house now. That's what she is about to do. Every step she took throbbed with joyful anticipation. They climbed the stairs. Fateema's house was an unplastered brick structure. She began to say to the walls, "I have struggled a lot to meet you. Bas, my home, we will soon be with each other!" She thought of her siblings and parents.

Her fingers caressed the walls. She came down the stairs and went into the site office. She had to pick up a copy of the agreement.

"Arre, what is the building called?"

"We were thinking of Sunrise Complex."

"Sunrise. That's great!"

With a copy in her hand, she came out. Her gaze kept going towards her house under construction. Her mind arranged the furniture inside the house. Balcony – only a rosebush. Yes. Overwhelmed, she began heading towards her vehicle.

"Fateemaji!" someone called her.

She stopped in her tracks. A young man came out of the site office. She didn't know him. He came closer.

"Fateemaji, you don't remember me. Perhaps my name is familiar to you. Shamsu."

Fateema shook her head. "Sorry, I am not able to…"

"Never mind. I was part of the gathering Kareembhai used to organize and…" He didn't finish. "I came there occasionally. Fateemaji, your advice to study was well taken. I have completed my Masters now. Two of my friends studied as well, Maashallah."

"Shamsu, that's wonderful news!"

"Listen, we came to know that you bought an apartment here. We wouldn't have come to know, but the place where the lawyer had gone to get the agreement typed is where one of my friends worked. He immediately told me. We met the builder, Tusharbhai, then. We persuaded him to sell three more houses to our families." Shamsu's face brimmed with joy. She stood listening with astonishment... Wires are connected, and sometimes you find the switch.

Shamsu pointed his finger towards the complex, "Builderbhai will raise a wall between these two buildings. So our building will be separate. Fateemaji, I have even thought of a name for our building. Chaand-Tara Society. How do you like it? Fateemaji, thanks to you, all of us got to buy a house here."

Shamsu left. Tears trickled down Fateema's face.

Arre, the house she had been pining for was gone from her yet again? She wanted to live with everybody else. She was not inimical to her quam, but why should she have to live with a label? The garden she had imagined between the two buildings was now a wall? To one side, Sunrise, and the other, Chaand-Tara...

Separate houses for Hindus and Muslims, a fence between them. A new one.

Fateema used to sing at the top of her voice with the entire class.

Hand in hand
Heart to heart
We run together
To a life of progress

We were supposed to hold hands in this country and progress together, why this fence then?

Fateema stared at the agreement. What should she do with this? Never mind if years went by seeking refuge, courting humiliation. She can't stay in a ghetto. She must return the agreement to Tushar. She saw Shamsu walking towards her. He seemed to fly in the air. He and his friends had got apartments because of her. They would be denied homes, if she returned the agreement.

Fateema, take the house. Living together will bring down the prejudice, ignorance and contempt and, of course, the fence.

Hand in hand
Heart to heart

Fateema put the agreement in her purse and kick-started her two-wheeler.